Pleasant View

A Novel

Dianne Zimmermann

Published BookCrafters, Parker, Colorado.
www.BookCrafters.net

*I dedicate this book to my friends
whose never-ending encouragement
drove me on when the going got tough.*

Acknowledgements

I wish to thank my family of friends for their interest and encouragement in all my writing endeavors; Pleasant View is my fourth book. And I wish to express special thanks to LA Mott for her encouragement, proofreading and editing skills.

Chapter One

"Oh, Robert, let's get this red one," squealed Judy grinning from ear to ear as she glided about and circled the shinning vehicle, like a hungry soaring hawk aiming to pounce on unsuspecting prey. The brand new 1988 Cadillac Deville convertible was proudly featured by the dealership. Its classic smooth lines and brilliant red paint and chrome trim brilliantly displayed under the main showroom spotlights. The convertible's front grill appeared to smile invitingly with top down appeal, alluring Judy and calling to her material girl instincts.

She loved bright shining things, as was evident by her bright red hair, glittery green eye shadow, matching her green eyes, framed by long luscious thick eyelashes, that fluttered when she flirted with her husband. Robert smiled as he watched his twirling wife with adoring eyes, as she joyfully jumped into the drivers seat and pretended to be driving the car and looking all around. He had to smile, she is a pleasant view, heaven to his eyes, and he was totally under her spell.

But, he had to admit, that Judy wanting such a fancy car, made him a bit nervous. *This too will cost me a bundle*, thought Robert as he smiled trying to share his wife's enthusiasm. Judy had expensive tastes; he knew that when he met her on her first day at work as he watched her eyeball the top executives stroll by wearing expensive tailored suits.

Why she settled for him, he never fully understood, because she could have gotten anyone of them. Perhaps she felt he was someone she could groom and dress up in all the latest fashions. Whatever the reason, he was crazy about her and wanted her love.

He smiled as he watched her get out from behind the wheel and dance around as she flirted with him. She knew her flirting drove him wild with desire. Especially today, he thought, his wife looked exceptionally sexy as she wore black stretch stirrup pants with a pink turtle neck sweater. That accentuated her sparkling personality, as did her red hair stacked high in curls above her head. Earrings dangled, bangle bracelets jangled in holiday style, as she danced and slid in and out the fancy car.

Every day was Christmas for Judy when she had her heart set on something! She tugged on Robert's arm and looked dreamily into his eyes, watching any resistance he may have had weaken and slip away with each touch, as she clung to him. Judy always got what she wanted, because she was Robert's muse to success and riches, and he knew it. He was reluctant to spend large amounts of money before he met Judy, some even calling him a miser. But Judy changed all that and convinced him to let loose of his money once in a while. He knew her wishes for riches would inspire him and he would one day build an empire of wealth around her.

"You have to dress for success, must I remind you, time after time?" Judy would sing the words, "Time after time" and she sounded just like her idol Cyndi Lauper. Looking good was very important to Judy. She loved the way people looked at them wherever they went. It took a bit of doing; but Judy finally convinced Robert to dress impeccably in Giorgio Armani fashion.

"You look so handsome," Judy flirted as she danced up to him and straightened his tie and sang Cyndi Lauper's "Girls Just Want to Have Fun," and kissed him. Robert adored her not so unique look for she looked and dressed like Cyndi Lauper and spent money like Madonna's "Material Girl."

"Anything your little heart desires darling." Robert smiled as the salesman approached them and introduced himself.

"Hi, the name's George," the salesman said as he extended his hand in a kind and gentle greeting to Judy. He then turned his attention to Robert and shook his hand with the firm vigor of an authoritarian man-to-man grip. He looked Robert in the eye and smiled as if to confirm that he knew that Robert was the man of the house.

George had seen it many times when husbands and wives came into the dealership. He knew that when the wife was along, it almost guaranteed sale. *What men won't do to keep their wives happy!* thought George.

"Oh, it's a beauty, isn't it?" George smiled then went on to describe the car's fancy features: This 1988 Cadillac Deville convertible is a real beauty all right! It has a high-tech General Motors touring suspension, a sweet 4.5 liter V-8 engine, 22 miles per gallon on the highway, hydro-super glide transmission, fifteen inch alloy wheels, special leather seats, rear sway bar and a special tighter steering ratio for enhanced handling," announced George in one breath, proudly smiling as he looked at the car then at the promising faces of the couple standing before him, although they looked a little puzzled.

None of what the salesman described about the car meant anything to Judy, or Robert for that matter. They just smiled and nodded their heads as neither was very mechanically inclined. George addressed Robert when he spoke about the mechanical features of the car. He showed the little lady the power seats, cassette drive and push button radio features.

Judy smiled and immediately reached in her big hot pink purse and pulled out a cassette tape and smiled as she listened to high tech speakers: "living in a material world, and I am a material girl..." So, fitting," Judy thought. She was lost in a daydream, fantasizing about turning admiring heads, as she drove around town in a brand new shinning red Cadillac Deville convertible.

She was oblivious to George's awarding winning sales spiel; that is, until he got to talking about executives and dignitaries.

George was the highest volume-selling salesman in the dealership. His egotistical personally was further enhanced when he won an award for his savvy salesman techniques. He dedicated his accomplishments to his talented imagination, for he could spread a line of bull a mile long. He knew these two potential customers, especially the wife, were all about the importance of impressing people. So, he gave them a bonus of his best sales pitch spiel ever.

"Oh yes, she's a real beauty all right," bragged George, "a real one of a kind, beauty." George couldn't help but grin; he had their full attention, so he then threw out his self-proclaimed game winning fast pitch curve ball: "Folks you are in for a treat!"

George smiled showing his newly capped pearly-whites. He was excited about this potential sale. Yet, he was a bit nervous; there was always a chance of losing a sale. He ran his hand threw his thick curly heavily-dyed black hair that was so dull and damaged from over coloring that it had the look of suede. He was so proud because he dyed it himself, even smeared a little dab on his eyebrows.

He knew the man's wife was staring at him because he looked so handsome. He wore his best white short sleeve shirt, the one with the least frayed collar. He sported a brown and pink paisley necktie, and wore his favorite brown and pink plaid trousers that day. His luckiest pair of pants, that made his butt look good. He always made a sale when he wore them.

George knew he was a hit! He stuck to his award winning perfectly memorized spiel just as he practiced it. He saw that Judy and Robert were intrigued and so continued, giving them the long version.

"This particular model is one of a limited-edition production models that was specifically designed and produced for selected General Motors executives, top shareholders, and a short list of dignitaries." George smiled as their eyes lit up. He knew he had them. Going in for the kill, he added what he knew would clinch the deal.

"The manufacturer only released a handful of these gorgeous beauties for sale to the public," George boasted. He watched their pretentious smiles grow ever larger. "This particular car is the last one for sale in a hundred-mile radius."

"Oh my!" Judy could barely contain herself at the thought of owning a rare one-of-a-kind Cadillac.

"This is your lucky day," George said. He knew he had them in his clutches when he saw their eyes light up at the thought of owning something bright red and showy that no one else had.

Having a special limited edition Cadillac was music to Judy and Robert's flamboyant ears. They smiled, looked at each other, nodded, then turned to George and in unison announced, "We'll take it!"

The words lingered in the air for a moment, but even longer in Robert's brain. What was he doing? For a brief moment, Robert's brain went into a frantic tailspin as he rapidly calculated numbers in his head trying to figure out how he was going to actually pay for such an expensive automobile. A sharp tightness gripped his gut for a moment; that is, until he reminded himself that he was soon to become a very wealthy man. He had no worries.

Robert, enabled and encouraged by his muse, Judy, had just built a huge retirement community called Pleasant View. It was named that, not only for the beautiful oasis in the desert view that surrounded the building, but because Judy was Robert's most pleasant view. Wealth was assured as residents came pouring in and bringing with them their retirement savings accounts for him to manage.

Demographically, as America was aging, he felt that he was creating a much-needed service for aging seniors. The senior living center provided not only housing, but also portfolio investment management, complete medical care and rehab units, and an upscale restaurant.

So, yes, he convinced himself that he could easily afford an expensive automobile. Besides, as Judy reminded him, an aspiring businessman needs to advertise his success in order to attract more investors. Robert was on his way to becoming as successful as his father had been.

If only his dad could see him now, he thought.

CHAPTER TWO

Robert's father had been strict with him while Robert was growing up. He was very business minded and pushed Robert to succeed at all cost, in whatever endeavor he pursued. Failure was not an option.

Judy had the same adventurous spirit Robert's father had, and comfortably filled his father's shoes as Robert's mentor and muse. She was just the extra push he needed, just as his father had pushed him; right up to the moment he died. Doctors had said his father's failed heart was a result of his over-worked hyperactive type-A personality. Robert was not afraid that a bad heart would cause his death. Anyway, he would risk it, he thought. He wanted to be just as successful as his father wanted him to be and as Judy wanted him to be.

****

Robert just knew that his dad was looking down and smiling on him, as he drove out of the dealership and headed down the busiest street in Tucson, for everyone to see them. The top was down, and Robert proudly held Judy's hand as they drove. The sun was shining as they cruised along, slithering in and out of traffic, meandering amongst the bustling crowds of shoppers, and business people going about their day.

Robert smiled and nodded to the people who stared at them. He felt as if they actually were dignitaries in a highfalutin' parade. Judy grinned as she saw their reflection in the storefront windows as they passed by. She had to admit, they were a beautiful couple.

Looking beyond their lovely reflections, she spotted a classic outfit on a mannequin in one of the storefront windows. She decided she needed a new outfit—something classic to match their classy limited-edition brand-new Cadillac. She noted the name of the dress shop and vowed that she would return for that sharp white wool suit with padded shoulders. Of course then she would need new shoes and handbag to go with the new suit. Buying this car had set her off and her mind was in a spending frenzy. In her crazy mind, Judy had to make up for lost time, for when she had felt poor.

Judy had come from a very humble background. Her mother went to work as a waitress, cleaned houses, and even became a seamstress, after her loving husband died in a foundry accident where he worked. Judy was ten years old. Judy was her mother's only child and very precious and spoiled. Her mother worked long hours in order to buy Judy the most expensive clothes and all the Barbie dolls that she wanted. As Judy grew older and hung out with the rich kids at school her tastes grew even more expensive.

Judy had always felt deprived as a kid by her loving father's untimely passing. She grew up with an ache in her heart and a vow to marry a rich man. To Judy, men were the way to all the material things she wanted. She worked in the financial sector to meet young aspiring businessmen.

Judy met Robert when she began work as a financial secretary at the investment firm. It was pretend love at first sight for her. Robert was tall dark and handsome and made lot of money. She giggled and flirted with him. He was flattered beyond belief that such a spunky cute girl would even be interested in him. Robert was shy and charming and talk around the office water cooler was that he was the most aspiring agent in the investment pool, so Judy set her sights on him. With a little sexual persuasion on her part, shy conservative Robert was as good as hers.

It was a speedy courtship and Judy and Robert married within one year after they met. They had a small but expensive wedding with only a few friends invited from work. Judy was an only child as was Robert, so no family to speak of for either of them. Judy's mother, who had worked so hard to give Judy everything she wanted, died from cancer, several years earlier. Robert's only family member, his mother, Marie, attended the reception. His grandmother was in the nursing home and unable to be there.

Marie enjoyed herself immensely as she danced with Robert, some of his co-workers, and with Ann, her best friend, visiting from Sedona. They all enjoyed the elaborate country club setting, a lovely dinner and danced the evening away.

CHAPTER THREE

Robert and Judy's wedding celebration was a delight for them as well as everyone who attended the joyous occasion. And it had been the first time in a long time that Marie got a chance to kick up her heels a bit. She didn't get a chance to socialize much the two years that Frank, Robert's father, was ill, so she was having the time of her life at the reception.

Marie was a devoted wife and never left her husband's side for more than an hour or two, to run errands, and only while the visiting nurse was there. She loved her husband but felt imprisoned by duty, and then she felt guilty for feeling that way. It was a tough couple of years.

After Frank died, she felt like a free bird that needed to fly away. So she would frequently visit her longtime friend, Ann, in Sedona, a mere four-hour drive from Tucson. Ann had always been a dear friend whom she kept in touch with through the years—through thick and thin. Marie was there for Ann through her divorce and Ann was there for Marie through Frank's illness. They supported each other when both of their sets of parents suffered fading health and when they passed. Neither could believe it had been so many years.

Ann tried to convince Marie that she would love living in Sedona with the wonderful vortex energy of the red rock mountains that surrounded the city. Ann had moved to Sedona after she retired from a government job in Washington D.C. with the Federal Bureau of Investigation.

She had always loved Sedona ever since she had vacationed at a spiritual health resort there after her troublesome divorce. The moment she arrived and saw the surrounding beauty, she fell in love with the red rocks and the wonderful vortex energy she felt there. And so she fulfilled her promise to herself to move there after she retired.

Sedona felt just right for a new beginning and a fresh start. Ann lived in a condominium community surrounded by huge red rocks that Sedona is famously known for. She had a pleasant view of Coffee Pot Rock from her patio.

Marie would come and visit; she enjoyed visiting Ann and feeling the magical vortex of the red rocks. They enjoyed coffee and breakfast on the patio before they went hiking in the morning, and sipping gin and tonics before dinner. Ann had warned Marie that Sedona would call her back if she came to visit, and it did. The magical majestic red mountains did indeed call her back after her fist visit and so she visited several times a year. Marie was fond of Ann. They had discovered common interest when they met in a special one-time investigative journalism class, presented by the English department in their teenage high school many years earlier.

Marie had been a little jealous and sad that her life path took a turn from a career in journalism to a stay-at-home mom. So, Marie enjoyed living vicariously through Ann's exciting career and listening to the investigative stories she shared. Wife and mother were supposed to be the major life course for every woman, Marie's mother always said. But Marie wanted a professional career.

Marie thought that she could work and pursue her career when Robert got old enough to go to school but when the time came, Frank wouldn't hear of her going to work. She knew she could have done both, take care of things at home, and still go to work every day, many women did. Frank had been encouraging about her pursuing her career before they married, but after they married, and Robert came along, Frank said he didn't want her to go to work.

She was disappointed but felt she thought maybe he was right and decided to honor his wishes. She would discuss it with Ann. Ann was always there for her and very understanding and listened intently while Marie unleashed her thoughts and pent up anxiety.

"You are so understanding," said Marie filled with gratitude, "what would I ever do without you?"

"Well, Marie," admitted Ann, "you have also always been there for me through my tough times with my career and my troubles with Joe, before we divorced. So, we are kind of even."

Marie loved spending time with Ann who was as vibrant and active as Marie, now in her early seventies. They hiked the many trails near Sedona around Bell Rock, Cathedral Rock, and Boynton Canyon. They enjoyed each other's company and hiked well together, taking on challenging trails that involved climbing on and over huge rock formations at the base of the mountains.

Everyone they met thought Ann and Marie were sisters. They looked a lot alike; both were tall and thin with silver hair, and lovely smiles. Ann wanted Marie to move to Sedona and tried her best to persuade her to move there every time she visited.

"You need to move to Sedona," insisted Ann and invited her to move in with her. Marie thought about taking Ann up on her offer every time she visited her; but, just as if it were clockwork, she would then get a call from her son Robert.

"How are you, Mother?" asked Robert. "Are you ready to come home?"

"Soon son, soon," Marie would respond. She didn't really want to go home, but then the guilt would set in. As it was, Marie never stayed for more than a week because Robert, without fail, would call wanting her to come back home. Marie could count on his calls if she wasn't back home after one week. He insisted he missed her.

Robert became over protective of his mother after his father died and wanted his mother close by so he could keep an eye on her. Marie was torn between doing what she wanted to do and honoring Robert's wishes. To keep peace with her son, Marie would remain living in Tucson under the watchful eye of her doting son, who seemed to grow more like his father each day. Marie actually thought she would be able to enjoy so much more freedom after Frank had died, but she knew she was somehow repeating a pattern with her son.

"You would think I was some old, decrepit woman, or something," Marie would complain to Ann. Ann encouraged Marie to ignore her possessive son's wishes, but Marie remained true to her promise to Robert and only made short visits to Sedona throughout the year.

CHAPTER FOUR

In her youth, freedom-loving Marie had her heart set on a professional career. She had not planned to marry at all. But circumstances forced her into marriage and motherhood. Of course, she loved her son, Robert. And she had to admit she loved her husband. Frank started out being a very loving husband and father, but later something changed, and he became very possessive and demanding, always wanting to know her whereabouts. He wanted her at his beck and call every minute of the day.

Marie still dreamed of having an investigative journalist career. When Robert was old enough to go to school she wanted to go work and thought that Frank would support her decision, and be proud of her. But to her disappointment, he took quite the opposite stance to her wishes and insisted she be at home for Robert.

Frank called Marie several times a day wanting to know what she was doing. One would think that this constant supervision would give Marie the sense of being greatly loved, but rather it made her feel trapped and owned. To Marie, Frank's possessiveness felt more like a watch dog dogging her, a border collie nipping at her heels to keep her in her space that he allowed her to be in.

He expected her to run errands for him and have dinner on the table when he got home. He controlled her social life, or lack of one, and limited her friends to his associate friends.

Frank had what doctors called a type-A personality that contributed to his heart disease. He was high-strung and worked twelve hours a day. He could never make enough money to suit himself. Marie used to worry about his health and would suggest that he slow down. Of course, he would not listen to her. Marie decided that he was just a typical patriarch authoritarian just as his father and her father had been, which probably led to their early deaths.

Marie's father had been a pillar of the community. He served on the school board; he was an active member of their church and an investment broker for the congregation and neighboring communities. Of course, her father approved of Frank the moment he met him, because Frank was just like him. When Marie had doubts about marrying Frank, her father egged her on, because he thought that Frank would be the perfect husband for her.

Men always know best, her mother would say. Marie was a silent partner just as her mother had been a silent partner to her father always agreeing and holding all emotions inside.

Her mother took care of Marie's dad until he died. Marie thought that was why her mother got sick. Her mother suffered through several surgeries. Marie knew first hand her mother's suffering, because when she could no longer live alone, Marie moved her in with her and Frank.

Frank couldn't bear to listen to her constant complaining, and worked even longer hours, never relieving Marie, who was a constant fixture at her mother's bedside. When her mother became too ill for Marie to take care of her, Marie had to put her in a nursing home, which Marie hated doing. Her mother hated it even more and did not go easily, and fought it every step of the way.

Marie was suffocating between her dealings with her cantankerous mother, and her difficult marriage that she too thought she would die of an illness brought on by stifled emotions. She longed for some independence. Again, Marie wanted to get out and go to work. But Frank worried about his status in the community. What would people think if his wife had to go to work? If Marie went to work it would appear that he was not successful enough to support his wife and their upper middle-class lifestyle.

Appearances were everything to Frank. He had to appear successful even if it meant cooking the books from time to time, when times were tough, and he needed to show a profit in a slow month. Frank had to win; there was no such thing as losing. It was the way his father did business and the way he taught his son to do business.

As time went on, the stress of his competitive lifestyle wore on his health. He pushed himself until one day, two years to the day after Marie's mother passed, he suffered a massive heart attack and Marie was confined to his bedside, to take care of him. Frank was put on a multitude of drugs. Gradually his strength grew a little better, and his daily routine consisted of slow walks around the house. He pressed on always demanding his doctor do more.

So one day his doctor put him on a new experimental drug. It seemed to help for a while, but then only hastened the path to Frank's demise. Frank suddenly lost consciousness after taking the medicine only a short while. He was rushed to the hospital where doctors took him off the drug and monitored his progress. He recovered enough to go home, but total bed rest was required. Several weeks later he died in his sleep.

Frank's death was a relief to Marie. She had been his constant caregiver for over two years, a tough demanding job take took every minute of her day to answer his constant demands. Once again, as with her mother, she had felt like a prisoner in her own home. Of course, she was ashamed to admit that to herself or anyone else.

She found herself lost. She didn't know how to act on her own and didn't know what she wanted to do next. It took her a while to adjust, to her new-found freedom, because the walls still seemed to echo his constant demands.

"Bring me some fresh water," he would order in a strong voice. So strong that Marie thought he could get up out of bed and get it himself. Of course, then she would feel guilty that the sound of his voice made her cringe. He wouldn't ask for things in a polite way; but rather, he would order her. And while she was getting fresh water for him, before she got back with it, he had thought of something else he wanted her to run and get for him. Marie ran back and forth like that all day.

She could see that he enjoyed seeing her wait on him hand and foot. He preferred she sit on a chair next to his bed day and night, much like her mother did, to keep him company and answer his every whim. He had suffocated the life right out of her. Frank's main concern was himself and his reputation. The past haunted her and although she tried not to think of it, old memories cluttered her mind, especially on Robert's birthday. Robert had just turned fifty years old, a milestone for him as well as for Marie.

It was fifty years ago when Marie went to the doctors feeling nausea. She was seventeen when Frank and she had sex. She was worried about being pregnant. A girlfriend told her that she couldn't get pregnant just doing it one time; anyway she had never gotten pregnant after she and her boyfriend did it, but Marie did. Marie was stunned to learn the news, when she went to the doctor complaining with daily upset stomach. Her mother never told her ahead of time about periods or about the birds and bees, or anything of that nature. What little she learned she learned from the other girls at school. After she left the doctor's office, the doctor called the house and spoke to her mother. So, when Marie got home from school she was confronted with the shock of her life.

"You are pregnant! You have two options," her mother briskly commanded, "either marry Frank or we will send you away for nine months to the nun's convent where all young unwedded girls go to have their babies and give them up for adoption.

"He's a good man," her father said, "so if he is willing to marry you, you must get married." There was a term for a wedding in this type of situation—a shotgun wedding.

Marie was stunned! She didn't mention a word to anyone. She knew that her friends were all talking about her—how she got-in-trouble! How she got caught! The "loose" girl was always stuck with the blame, it seemed. Boys will be boys of course, and were never blamed. It was never shameful for boys, as if everyone knew that boys had no control over their impulses and desires.

Marie felt the shame and disappointment. She wasn't sure if she even was in love with Frank; much less, ready to marry him. She felt that she wasn't ready for marriage and the responsibility that came with being a wife and mother. Personally, she thought that she would have preferred nine months at the convent and then adoption. But she knew that Frank, and her mother and father would never hear of it.

"What would people think?" her mother said. She was so worried about what people would think and not how Marie felt or what she thought. Marie was disappointed in herself and mad at Frank for putting her in this position. She wondered, did Frank actually want to get her pregnant, to trap her into marriage? It sure would have been one way to keep her for himself, and from pursuing her career in journalism.

Marie was also afraid her whole world would never be the same again. She knew that telling Frank would be the beginning that would change her life forever. Just as she figured, Frank seemed to know she was pregnant even before she broke the news to him. Frank was actually excited and insisted they get married right away. Marie was dubious about marriage at this point in her life. She thought that maybe someday she would be ready, but not now. It didn't help her situation that her parents liked Frank and were excited that he wanted to get married right away. They said lots of girls get married at a young age and babies do come early sometimes.

It was 1938, she was pregnant and not real thrilled about it. She liked Frank well enough, even thought she loved him. Frank was also concerned, he was an up and coming promising business man in the community and did not take kindly to idle gossip, especially concerning his reputation, so she and Frank married as soon as possible.

Marie knew that Frank would be a good financial provider for her and their baby. He liked his accountant job at the bank, and it paid well. He picked out a house and put a down payment on it and then surprised her with it. She was disappointed that she had no hand in the decision. He did the same when he bought the family car, he picked it out. Again she was disappointed and thought that she should have had a say in the decision.

When she complained about it, her mother told her that men know better about those things. Frank knew what it took to keep up with the Jones; appearances were everything when you were a promising junior accountant at one of the largest banks in the community. He would raise their son to be just like him.

CHAPTER FIVE

Their beautiful son was born nine months to the day after they got married. They named him Robert, after Frank's dad. They were proud parents. Frank adored him, as did Marie. Motherhood changes everything and Marie loved being a mother and wondered how she ever had thoughts of giving him up for adoption.

Robert was her happiness and Marie soon settled in to caring and being happy with her little family. She participated in school and church activities, and became secretary of both organizations. Frank was okay with this, because volunteer work at the school and the church, is what professional men's wives were expected to do. So Marie too became concerned, just as her mother was, about what people thought.

Marie, Frank and Robert, lived in a lovely stucco ranch house complete with several mesquite trees, cacti, with a pleasant view of the Santa Rita Mountains.

The rising foothills could be seen just outside their subdivision that was situated in an impressive up-and-coming affluent neighborhood. The house was perfect for the three of them. They lived close to the bank where Frank worked, which was located near Robert's school. Every morning Frank walked Robert to school. They passed the bank on the way, sometimes they would stop in and Robert would visit with Frank's co-workers, then they would continue to walk one block further to Robert's school. Robert would hug his dad good-bye, and then Frank walked back to go to work at the bank.

Robert enjoyed their walks to school and the bank visits. He was proud of his father and wanted to be just like him. Their morning walks were bonding moments as Frank told Robert all about the banking business and persuaded Robert to study math and finance and to learn it well, so he too one day could be an accountant and a financial executive.

Marie's days became quite mundane. She spent her days taking care of matters around the house. She did the washing, cooking, cleaning and tending to her small garden. The garden alone kept her busy enough with weeding, picking and canning and preparing meals for Frank and Robert, so busy she did not have much time to think about her dream job of being a journalist. Marie loved her husband and son. Frank was domineering of course, but a good provider. Most importantly, Frank was a very supportive and loving father to Robert.

***

Robert was as smart as a whip, so school came easy for him. He was an excellent student. After college he became a Certified Public Accountant and worked as an investment banker much like his father. At work, Robert was ambitious and easily learned his job. He became fast friends with his co-workers, especially one, named Judy.

"You are such a pleasant view," Robert smiled and told Judy, each morning when he came into work and passed her desk. He loved the way she smiled, her red hair, and the bright happy colors she always wore.

"Why thank you Mr. Dems," she would flirt back.

Judy was the new girl in the office and proved to be business savvy and very ambitious. Judy was hired on as a teller, right after her bankrupted investment broker husband, Roger, was killed in a tragic auto accident. Judy said Roger was reckless and always drove too fast. One morning after an argument with Judy, he stormed out of the house, got in is car and raced down the mountainside even faster then what he normally drove.

He was upset, because Judy was upset that he had lost all of their money in bad investments. To police, it appeared that he took the winding mountain road down from their house much too fast and lost control of the car and crashed through the guardrail barrier and landed in the deep careen below.

Judy wasn't a widow for long. She was a big flirt and soon she and Robert began dating. It wasn't long before they were engaged, and within a few months' time, Robert and Judy got married.

CHAPTER SIX

arie loved her son; but as hard as she tried, she
could not manage to grow fond of her daughter-
in-law. Fact was, Marie was not at all fond of Judy. Marie
thought Judy was nothing more than a money hungry
gold digger, after Robert for his money. Marie told herself
it was only her imagination, and that most mothers feel
there is no woman good enough for their son.

But, no matter what Marie thought, she kept it to
herself because Robert was crazy about Judy. Theirs
was a whirlwind romance; Judy swept Robert off his
feet. Before he knew it, he was proposing and she was
planning an extravagant wedding at the country club
she made him join.

All highly successful professionals, Judy told Robert,
belonged to the country club and that was where the
wedding reception should be held. Judy insisted on the
best of everything and she persuaded Robert that they
should mingle amongst the elite of the community.

They were up and coming affluent people; so, their wedding had to be very elegant. Of course, Judy had to have the most expensive Christian Dior wedding gown. Judy insisted she knew best what Marie should wear and frowned at the dress that Marie had picked out.

Judy picked out Marie's dress for the wedding because it had to be just so. Judy picked a long flowing, depressingly bland gray dress for Marie. Marie was a very attractive woman and there was no way that she going to outshine Judy. Marie thought the dress was very unattractive, and of course, very expensive. But Judy insisted it had to be the one she wanted Marie to wear. Marie bought it but she thought that the color made her look ill and the style made her look dumpy. Marie was depressed because she thought that she had looked stunning in the dress she had chosen and told Judy she wanted. It was a beautiful light blue shade with smooth easy flowing lines that made her look slim, tan, and highlighted her blue eyes.

But, Marie had to let it go. After all it was Judy's wedding, spoiled-rotten, brat, Judy's wedding—and Robert's too, of course. Robert adored Judy and she always got her way. Judy picked out the car, had a say in the house they lived in, and Judy always managed to get her way with Robert. Frank never allowed Marie to have a say in anything. And yes, Marie was jealous.

The house Robert had picked out wasn't quite big enough for Judy's taste. She had her eye on another one, a much bigger one. Robert, being madly in love with Judy, was determined to please her. With much discussion with the chief executive officer at the bank, he found a way to get an extended employee's loan, and so Judy got her perfect house in the nicer neighborhood, in a newer upscale subdivision. Judy was delighted she got her house, but totally disappointed with the interior so everything had to be redone. So there were remodeling expenses to cover.

Robert sucked it up and managed to shell out more money for the interior designer guy that Judy thought she needed. The cost, of course ran higher, then Robert expected, when the designer, after several attempts, finally got the colors of the drapes and carpet right. And after he got the furniture, she had ultimately decided upon. Of course she had to rearrange it, he didn't have it set up to her liking. In the end, even though she paid the designer to do it, she actually designed the whole house herself by telling the designer what to do and how to do it.

But the important thing was that she was pleased, and that was all that mattered. So what if anyone else thought the house was too colorful and bright. It only mattered that she and she alone, admired the beauty of her own artistic creations. To Judy, her house was a showcase, and she and Robert hosted many dinner parties to show it off.

Guests pretended to love the combination of bright colors of the rug and the drapes. The bright chartreuse and purple, the various shades of red, orange and yellows that were displayed proudly by Judy, and falsely admired by guests, who walked throughout the house a gasped, holding their hands over their mouths in disbelief. When asked, some would describe her taste as eclectic, bizarre, a little unusual, very unusual, and very busy and bright. Judy loved her unique decorative displays and thought they were brilliant. Robert was happy as long as Judy was happy and as long as he didn't think about how much it all cost him.

Judy was as busy and brilliant as her taste and being so, of course, she thought that Robert should be more like her. So she pressed Robert to prepare for a promotion to become vice-president. She encouraged him to learn the ropes of the position so he could be ready when a prestigious position presented itself. He told Judy that he wanted to climb the ladder of success; but he was really doing it mostly to please her. Robert was tired. He was tired from trying to keep up with Judy. Instinctively, he wasn't as ambitious as his father always wanted him to be, or as Judy wanted him to be.

Robert pushed himself, remained diligent and worked hard so It didn't take him long to climb the next promotional rung of the ladder. He moved up from loan officer to vice-president of the business real estate investment department. Judy was happy with his promotion, but Robert felt a little out of his element. He felt daunted with all the high ranked talent that surrounded him and it stressed him. Of course, Judy didn't notice that Robert began to look drawn and tired and lacked energy. Judy didn't notice or paid him no mind; however, his mother thought Robert looked ragged.

Marie noticed Robert's lack of enthusiasm. It wasn't long before she could see that Robert had dark circles under his eyes, was getting thin and losing his hair. Did she dare say something to Judy? She pondered the thought to keep quiet; but, then gave into it and said something to Judy about Robert's health. Angered by the insinuation that she was not taking good care of her husband, but skilled in conniving and manipulating, and wanting to appear polite and cordial, Judy merely laughed a slight forced laugh and smiled.

"Oh, that's Robert, all right, rugged," she said.

"I'm just a little worried…" Marie said expressing concern, but before she could finish Judy cut her off.

"He's just getting older," snapped Judy, then remembered to control herself and added, "I think he looks distinguished, don't you?"

She was wishing that annoying, nosy, Marie would just mind her own business. She told Marie that she had Robert on a healthy diet and that was why he was a little thinner. She contributed his graying and thinning hair to just getting older. She didn't mention the dark circles.

"Well, I'm worried about him," Marie repeated to death ears, because Judy had already shut her out. Marie convinced herself that Judy could have cared less about Robert; she did care about how much money he made, however.

"Well, I like the more distinguished look," Judy said with a smile, and she meant it. To her, Robert looked like an experienced vice-president should look. Marie, on the other hand, thought that Robert looked and acted like he was about to have a nervous breakdown. He was sweaty, red faced and his hands had a slight tremor to them. But in order to keep peace, Marie kept any further thoughts and concerns about Robert to herself. She did not want to start any trouble with Judy, for Robert's sake. She was more than aware that her son had a right to love and marry whomever he chose. Marie just had to get used to stepping aside and letting go, certainly through the years she only too well learned how to do just that.

When she was very young, Marie came to realize that letting go was a big part of life. She had to let go of the idea of having a warm loving mother, of having to let go of her dream career at a very young age when she got pregnant and married Frank; of letting go when her parents passed on; of having to let go when her son grew up and went off to college; of having to let go of the idea of returning to pursue her journalistic career. But the hardest lesson to learn, and to let go, was when her only son married a lunatic.

CHAPTER SEVEN

Judy was a lunatic all right, one that saw dollar signs when Robert had brought her along with him to the nursing home to visit his grandmother. She saw an opportunity to exploit senior citizens. She remembered how Marie took care of her mother in her home, saw how tough it was trying to deal with the endless demands.

The situation was difficult enough, but made worse, when Marie's mother fell and broke her hip. After breaking her hip and a brief hospital stay, Marie's mother went directly to a nursing home, much to her mother's endless protest. Marie's cantankerous mother was not at all happy caged in a depressing nursing home, and pontificated that fact each day by protesting from morning to night.

Nothing there was right for her. The food was tasteless and didn't sit well. And when she complained that the help was crabby and bossy that is, if and when they decided to show up to her room after she rang for them, over and over again. A daily litany of complaints about bad food, poor service, dirty rooms, was what Marie had to look forward to hearing about each day. Of course, young and cute Judy and Robert chimed right in with grandma whenever they visited her. Like grandma, they too were appalled at the sight of the ill equipped and shabby facility. Judy, always looking for a way to make money realized this might be another way to level up in the financial world; she and Robert could further their riches and investments by building a bigger and better senior living center.

"Robert, you know you could build a much better facility for your grandmother and others like her to enjoy," Judy eagerly suggested. "And you know your grandmother would be proud and happy to live in her grandson's wonderful facility." She encouraged him. In fact, Judy had her own ideas, and told Robert it could be a senior living center equipped with an urgent care medical staff, rehab facility, memory care and a nursing care. Robert liked the idea.

"What shall we name it?" asked Robert.

"I think I'm going to leave that up to you," Judy said, and laughed. She thought it was just like him to think of the name and not realize all the other elements that would go into a project like that.

"How about Pleasant View?" asked Robert. Judy was Robert's "Pleasant View," he always told her, and he wanted to name it after her.

Judy and Robert presented their brilliant idea living center to Robert's grandmother. She loved the idea and so stopped complaining when loving Robert and sweet little Judy came to visit, because she knew they were going to build a special living center just for her. But poor Marie remained a constant target of her mother's outburst and complaints.

"God will get you for putting me in this place," snorted Marie's mother when Marie came to visit her each day. Marie's mother complained to staff and told Marie about everything she thought was wrong there. It seemed no one could do anything right for Marie's mother. Of course, Robert and Judy got praised when they showed up. He was the apple of his grandmother's eye. The whole situation was a very exhausting to Marie. Just another thing she had to learn to let go of and accept as just part of life.

CHAPTER EIGHT

Although, Judy and Robert hurried to build Pleasant View Senior Living Center, grandma died just before the grand opening. She never got to see the grand project she inspired Judy and Robert to undertake. Judy thought that Marie should be more than happy to move there when the time came.

With both Mother and Frank gone. Marie finally had some breathing room. She was beginning to feel free to be herself, not someone's daughter, wife or mother. Marie had time to take some journalism classes at the community college. She loved it. She enjoyed her newfound independence of coming; going and choosing to do the things she wanted to do. She enjoyed taking classes, going on day trips and visiting her good friend Ann in Sedona. With her life becoming so active, Marie thought about downsizing to a condo.

There was too much always to do with taking care of a big house. Marie decided the house was just too big for her busy lifestyle and she began looking into selling her house and buying a small condo. Judy and Robert were not happy at all when they heard that Marie was thinking of using the money from the sale of her house to buy a condo. They thought she should sell her house and move into Pleasant View and bring all her money with her and have Robert invest and manage it.

Every time Robert and Judy visited Marie, they tried to encourage Marie to sell her house and move into Pleasant View. Robert and Judy told Marie that the current trend, besides paying the required money fees, in retirement centers, was to turn over all their savings and retirement money to the center to invest and manage. In that case, the center would handle all the resident's monetary concerns, thus contributing to the resident's carefree living experience. There were no monetary worries for seniors, as all expenses would come out of the lump sum they had turned over to Pleasant View. What was left when the resident passed into the spiritual realm would then be given to their designated survivors.

Marie did not like the idea of moving into an "old folks' home," as she called it. She had heard terrible stories about how people were ripped off and mistreated. Her own mother had been a prime example, as she had turned all her money over to where she was staying and paid two thousand a month for a small room and meals. All medicines and medical care was paid for per-needed service. Her mother had given over more than two hundred thousand to the home and by the time she died, there was barely enough left over for Marie to plan her funeral and burial.

Of course, Robert and Judy, being as greedy as they were, saw an opportunity to get their hands on some extra cash. So, they were all for taking over resident's large savings accounts to manage. And being as greedy as they were, they couldn't keep their hands off the money that was entrusted to them. And, so they began spending residents' money. Judy adjusted accounting records to show fake illnesses and reasons for lots of medications.

They advertised in daily newspapers and Pleasant View became very popular. There was a waiting list and as soon as someone died, the next person on the list quickly moved in. This was all fine and good, except Judy felt they weren't dying fast enough. She wanted a faster turnover in order to receive more lump suns of savings accounts. She shared those thoughts with an old friend who was a nurse at the facility. The two of them were of the same mind; some people lived too long for their own good. Robert would have been appalled if he had known. Robert was so busy he did not really know how the day to day operations worked at the facility.

Running the business was left to Judy and other administrators. Judy thought this could work well for them. They could have extra money to plan and build more senior living centers. Judy kept thinking they needed the revenue from the sale of Marie's house to get them well on their way. They both thought it would look good if Robert's mother lived in his brand-new facility. Advertising the fact might boost interest in potential residents.

But much to Robert and Judy's disappointment, Marie resisted their suggestions. She stuck to her plan to sell her house and use that money to buy a small condo either in Tucson or in Sedona where her friend Ann lived. Robert and Judy were very disappointed and unhappy when Marie shared her plans with them.

Marie was a vital woman who exercised daily. She was strong and healthy and could not see any reason to move to an assisted care facility. Marie was happy with her plans. She had finally finished her Liberal Arts Degree. A Bachelor's Degree was something she had always wanted and it made her feel special even if only she used it to check the "college degree" box on an application or a survey. It added to her sense of self and her sense of freedom to be her own person. She visited her friend Ann and they hiked the many trails surrounding the beautiful majestic red mountains surrounding Sedona. She was popular, gained lots of friends, and even dated a bit, which truly disturbed her son and his wife. They felt her dating any man dishonored the memory of Robert's father.

Robert, and especially Judy, protested because they were more afraid of Marie sharing her money with someone else besides them. Marie didn't argue, with them, she merely went on living her life, and enjoyed life doing what she pleased, but not totally without guilt. Being raised to please others, as she had been brought up, it was difficult for her to just do things for herself. She worried what her son thought and wanted to please him. And Robert like a good son, kept a close eye on his mother.

Robert called every few days to check on her like he had done for the past few years since his father died. And usually upon hearing what she had been up to, or thought of doing, he griped about it. It seemed she just couldn't do anything right in his eyes. Marie figured Judy influenced his thinking. At one point, Marie wanted to take a trip to Paris on a group tour, and she shared this dream plan with her son when he called one day.

"A trip to Paris?" he asked, "are you sure that is a good idea, Mother?"

"Well, yes, I do," smiled Marie in response." I thought you would be happy for me."

"But, what if you fall, got hurt, or got sick while you are over there?" he asked.

"It's bad enough that you are always trekking off to Sedona to see that friend of yours." Robert's voice lowered, as he complained. She could hear Judy in the background making comments, coaching him to convince his mother it would be silly to take an overseas trip. Robert was upset and couldn't figure out why his mother was always going against his wishes. Why could've she just be his mother and stay home like she did when he was growing up. Why couldn't she be content with seeing to his needs like she had always done for him and his father? He wanted her to stay put, so it would be easier for him to keep an eye on her.

Robert was also a little perturbed that his father's will had all his money go to his mother, and none was willed directly to him. He could not believe his father would believe a woman could handle that house and that much money. He thought he should have been taking care of his mother and her money. Plus, he was hoping for some of his father's money to go directly to him, so he could invest it, and not need to wait for his mother to pass to get it. Surely, she did not need that much money.

Marie tried to ignore the disappointment in Robert's voice, but she couldn't forget the way he sounded, and it depressed her. She could not understand his need to control her. Suddenly she didn't care about anything anymore. Robert had just taken the wind right out of her sails and the fun right out of her dream trip to Paris. Still, she vowed she would go anyway, someday.

Marie knew her money-hungry daughter-in-law, Judy, had a great influence in how Robert advised her. She knew that her son wished his father left some of the money he had to him, instead of leaving it all to her. Marie was doing her own monetary research; she merely wanted to be her own person and invest her money in mutual funds. She had a certain gut feeling about investing and it had always worked out well for her. She did her research and was pleased investing in reputable no-load mutual fund investments split with fifty-fifty stock market and bonds investments. She felt good about it. Her instincts were impeccable for within four years her investment gained nearly forty percent.

She kept good records, and she had a trust. Robert was her sole beneficiary.

One evening, at their weekly dinner at Marie's, while Marie was cooking and talking to Robert, Judy slipped away into Marie's office and snooped in Marie's files. There was only one small drawer of files and it was easy to read the folder names. Judy's eyes lit up when she came across the previous year's tax return and investment papers. She discovered that her mother-in-law was worth over a half-million dollars. Judy knew she and Robert would have so much more, after they sold Marie's house, which was paid for, free and clear.

Judy had encouraged Robert to invest and develop senior living communities. The plans were well thought out and included senior living, with associated assistant living when the time came, and also nursing home, pharmacy, rehab, and memory care to the complex. What attracted Robert and Judy, especially, was the idea that potential residents were encouraged to give all their money to the living center up front, the monthly fee of three thousand dollars plus health-aid expense would be automatically deducted from the lump sum.

There would be no monetary worries for the residents, nor Robert and Judy for that matter, to be concerned about. The idea was that the residents could live out their remaining days without any monetary worries. Contracts stated that when they passed, the remainder of the lump sum money they invested with Pleasant View would go directly to their beneficiaries listed in their contract. Judy knew it was a win—win situation for her and Robert. There was one problem; Judy felt they weren't getting their hands on residents' money fast enough. Judy lacked patience and wanted to get things moving faster than her mother-in-law was willing to move. Judy had her own plans, to speed events up a bit.

CHAPTER NINE

Marie invited Robert and Judy over for dinner every Sunday. In a way, it was Marie's way to show them that she was very capable of living in her own place, and how much she enjoyed her independence. She was tired of listening to them try to promote Pleasant View with all the pamphlets they left lying around her house on the coffee table and kitchen counters whenever they came over, but it became the norm.

One Sunday evening, dinner went fairly well as usual, as far as Robert and Judy's appetites went. Robert and Judy appeared to enjoy Marie's pot roast, as they ate every bit she cooked. Marie enjoyed their company but was rather surprised that there was none of Judy's usual sales pitch on this particular evening. She thought this was rather odd, but said nothing, grateful for the reprieve.

Instead, Judy and Robert brought up other topics of conversation; such as, movies, the weather, and politics,

Reagan, and what a fine job he was doing, firing the striking air control tower personal and hiring new ones, and demanding that the Berlin Wall come down. After the main course, they sat back and enjoyed coffee with lemon meringue pie that Judy and Robert brought with them. They knew lemon meringue was one of Marie's favorites.

"Such a treat!" thought Marie. She should have expected something was off right then and there, because normally Robert and Judy come empty handed. But still she enjoyed the pie and the company for the most part. It was good to spend time with Robert, and she tried to be pleasant with Judy, as Judy was being unusually very pleasant. All went very well until it was time to clear off the dining table after they were finished with desert. Judy helped Marie, which to Marie seemed almost too good to be true because normally Judy never lifted a finger to help. Usually, Judy sat in the living room on the sofa and read the paper while Marie gathered dishes and put things away.

But on this particular evening, Judy got up to help, much to Marie's surprise. Judy carried the water glasses, coffee cups and small plates the pie was served on to the sink. As Judy carried the water glasses, she purposely spilled a bit of water right on the ceramic tile floor in Marie's kitchen in a place where Marie would not see it. Marie came into the kitchen behind Judy, carrying the dirty dinner plates, and stepped into the spilled water. Marie came around the corner of the kitchen island, slipped on the spilled water and went down in a heap of crashing, chattering dishes. In one swift turn of events, she was spread out, lying on her back in pain, staring up at the ceiling.

Marie caught Judy's face as she stood nearby and watched the whole thing happen. Marie saw Judy's odd expression as she seemed to slide in slow motion down to the floor; she wondered about it as she passed out from the pain. Robert, who was in the bathroom at the time, came running into the kitchen to see what had happened after he heard the commotion. His eyes met Judy's and he saw the smirk on her face. *Did Judy deliberately trip his mother?* he wondered. Surely not! Robert felt a sudden cold chill! Many thoughts went through his mind at once.

Who was this woman standing before him, and just what was she capable of? The cute bubbly woman that he thought he knew was suddenly a stranger to him. *Who was she? He searched his mind and tried to remember just how Judy's first husband died, an accident of some sort? Oh yes, a car accident. Was he maliciously forced off the road, brakes lines cut? He tried to remember the details.*

Robert then turned to his mother when he heard her moan in pain as she tried to get up. He hesitated for a moment watching Judy, who stood there motionless and watched his mother struggle. Robert shook himself out of his thoughts and quickly stepped closer and bent down to get the dishes off of his mother and tried to help her up off the floor.

"Mother! Are you alright?" cried Robert with actual concern in his voice, consciously trying to cover up and compensate for what he was sure was Judy's evil deed. Judy just standing there and making no effort to help Marie get up, sent a message to Robert. Judy may have looked cute and innocent as her fashion hero, Cyndi Lauper, but her true colors were beginning to show, and Robert was beginning to see the real Judy underneath the flashy jewelry, colorful clothes and red hair piled high.

"Mother, are you hurt?" asked Robert again, in a low passionate tone, as he grabbed her hands and tried to pull her to her feet from sitting position.

"Wow, what happened?" Marie said rubbing her head she could feel a lump forming already. She felt like she had passed out for a few minutes, and she was a little dizzy. Shaken as she was, she looked herself and the kitchen over as she assessed the damage. She had a little cut on her hand from one of the broken dishes that flew out of her grip as her feet went out from under her.

She hadn't lost her balance or taken a fall since the first time she went hiking, among the red rocks of Sedona, with Ann. A memory flashed through her mind of her good friend, Ann, reaching down to pull her up. She missed Ann then, and wished she were with her now, to pull her up once again.

Robert's far-away sounding voice growing ever nearer brought her back to the present moment, as did the sudden sharp pain in her left ankle. Her head hurt, but her focus moved from her head, to her hand then to the spearing pain in her ankle.

"Ouch," she said as she sat back down and gave up

trying to get up onto her feet. Her ankle was beginning to swell.

"Where are you hurt?" Robert asked bending down her help her. Judy merely stood looking on, not moving or saying a thing.

"My ankle must to be sprained or, god-forbid, broken," complained Marie rubbing it as she sat on the floor.

"Come on, Mother, let's get you to urgent care," he said as he helped Marie to her feet.

Marie just wanted to sit a minute and catch her breath, but Judy had already found her purse and jacket and there was nothing to do but let Robert help her out. Judy walked slowly behind, following Robert as he helped Marie limp to her car. Judy put Marie's things in the back seat but did not get in. Marie had a little bit of trouble getting in the passenger side, it hurt, but she was eager to get her ankle taken care of so worked through the pain.

CHAPTER TEN

Robert drove his mother in her car to the Pleasant View urgent care facility. Judy remained behind at Marie's house to lock up she said; but really she wanted to stay behind in order to snoop around. She hurried to Marie's office desk and rummaged through all the files and documents she could find. She lingered over the ones regarding Marie's investments or anything of value Frank may have left behind. It took her a while to read through everything and make notes. She found papers that Frank's life insurance policy was quite generous at about a half a million and the house had to be at least worth two hundred thousand. When she finally felt she had searched through every possible file and drawer, she locked up the house and drove the shining red Cadillac convertible to join Robert and Marie at Pleasant View.

CHAPTER ELEVEN

Of course, Robert took his mother to Pleasant View's urgent care facility. It was close by and he owned it. Judy could not have planned it better. Her plan was to eventually talk his mother into moving in there; although Robert didn't look at it the same greedy way as Judy did, he was still influenced by her and believed she had good ideas. He let her make many of their decisions. Judy had convinced Robert that having his mother living in Pleasant View would be a huge selling point and what mother wouldn't want to live in her son's shining new center?

With Marie at Pleasant View as a patient, Judy's plan was in place. The Pleasant View doctor, Dr. Charles Allen, would be encouraged by Judy to suggest Marie stay in an apartment at the facility, so she could easily be wheeled to rehab each day. Robert was Marie's financial and healthcare power of attorney so he could make all the decisions.

With Marie out of the way, Judy's plan was to move forward with more intensity. Especially after she had read though Marie's financial and legal files and saw how much Marie was worth. Judy's next task was to convince Robert to put Marie's house on the market without telling Marie. It would be in Marie's best interest. After all, she was getting older and needed more care. All of Marie's assets would go to Pleasant View. Judy smiled and winked at Robert as she joined him and Marie. Robert wasn't sure what was going on in Judy's mind but that wink made him nervous. He was feeling a little anxious too about his mother's pain. It happened so fast.

"How is the ankle?" asked the nurse before giving Marie a shot for pain.

"Oh, this is nothing, just a little inconvenience," said Marie with a grimace as she tried to move it to get more comfortable. She tried to smile, she had never been a whiner and she was not about to start now; but, her ankle hurt like hell and so did her head. She didn't mention her headache to Robert, but she did hit her head on the floor. The fact that she had passed out momentarily sort of worried her, but she said nothing.

Marie wasn't used to being incapacitated and certainly not under her son and daughter-in-law's control. They had been so pushy about Pleasant View lately. She suddenly got a chill. She shook it off. There was nothing they could do while she was alive and conscious. She was used to being the caregiver. For the first time in her life she was beginning to feel vulnerable, weak. She hated to admit it, but even a little old. She tried to push those depressing thoughts away. It was a frightening wake-up call.

She was suddenly reminded that the course of your life could change in an instant from one of total independence to one of dependence and needing the help of others. Marie should have known, of course, that Judy saw her head hit the floor and said something to Robert as he helped her get into the car, adding conviction that she was indeed injured and needed tests—x-rays, CT scans and whatever.

Marie was beginning to feel more and more vulnerable by the minute. Worse than feeling vulnerable was the fear of being trapped under Robert and Judy's care. *She wished she had not made Robert full power of attorney regarding her wealth and healthcare—what was she thinking?* But, after Frank died, Robert and Judy had talked her into it.

Word spread fast that the center's owner, Robert Dems, and his mother were in Urgent Care. All personnel were on high alert. Dr. Charles Allen and a nurse appeared in an instant to attend to Marie. They took Marie's personal information followed by a litany of questions regarding previous and present conditions. What drugs was she taking? Was she experiencing headaches, was she nauseated, and on and on the questions continued. Marie answered as best as she could. She was not taking any prescription medications.

A new medical file including billing information was set up. An order for x-rays, and a CT scan soon followed. Marie was most nervous about the CT scan; the thought of being all closed up in that big tube-like capsule frightened her. The nurse assured her that she would be fine as she handed her a Valium and small cup of water. The pill would calm her nervousness, the nurse said. Normally, Marie would reject an offer of medications; but she was not having a good day, feeling vulnerable and weak, so she readily took the pill the nurse offered her.

This was the first time since she gave birth to Robert, over fifty years ago, that she felt so vulnerable and out of control of her circumstances. The pill had a fast effect and it wasn't long before Marie felt very relaxed, even woozy. The pill was very effective, and Marie found that the CT scan procedure was a sedated cinch. She was higher than a kite. She was ready for anything.

She didn't have to wait long before Dr. Allen came back with all the tests results. When he looked at the x-rays he told her she had a fracture to her left ankle, had a fracture on her left third metatarsal and she had a mild concussion.

"Funny, I don't feel a thing," insisted Marie grinning with a dazed look in her eyes. She was being truthful. She was so loaded up on the pain pills; she didn't feel a thing when Dr. Allen pressed around on her ankle and foot. When they were finished and satisfied that they had tested, poked and probed enough, the nurse gave her some more pills, helped her get in a wheelchair, and then wheeled her to her apartment. She was told that she would be staying at the center so she could go to rehab every day.

She had no idea what they said. She was so high and drugged up that she mumbled the fact that she was a healthy able woman and could just use the crutches and hobble on home. She thought that since it was her left foot, she would be able to drive her car. She was woozy, and the pills were making her feel a little paranoid. She was beginning to feel uneasy, but said nothing. She felt as if Robert, Judy, Dr. Allen and his staff were over-reacting to her minor injury by insisting she stay there. No matter, what they were up to, she was too doped up to protest. She knew they would not let her go home that night. Marie didn't see it, but Dr. Allen winked at Judy, as he told Marie that she had a concussion. Dr. Allen and Judy had succeeded, and had Marie right where Judy wanted her.

"Faster, faster!" Marie laughingly ordered the attendant who pushed her wheelchair. She was high on the Valium and pain pills they had given her and no longer cared about anything. The tests took quite a while and it was late by the time Marie was wheeled to her room. Robert and Judy had waited in Marie's room so when she arrived Judy had the apartment door wide open, so the attendant could easily wheel her in avoiding any possible resistance from Marie. There was no resistance, quite the contrary in fact.

"Hey, there," Marie smiled as if in a drunken stupor as Judy stepped aside.

"Hey there yourself," Judy smiled a winning smile.

She was happy. The attendant wheeled Marie around her new living quarters and then gave Marie the sedative Judy provided. Marie already high from the earlier medications easily took it. It would make her fall asleep soon, but she had a few minutes to look around before it took effect.

"Oh, my, look how lovely this is," exclaimed Marie, looking the place over and oohing and ahhing about the lovely new fixtures and furniture.

"It's lovely isn't it?" Judy replied. *Oh, the wonders of modern medicine*, she thought.

"Nice big window," Marie smiled then as she looked out added, "Pleasant view!" Then laughed at her own drunken-stupor wit. She wheeled herself to get a better look out the huge ceiling-to-floor window, which over looked the lovely landscaped grounds with various flowers and cacti everywhere. Lovely palm trees surrounded the lake and walking path. It was indeed a pleasant view.

Robert had reserved the best luxury apartment for his mother against Judy's better judgment. She thought that the luxury apartment should be reserved for a resident who brought the biggest bundle of cash with them. But, Judy quickly got over it, since she was now in full control of Marie and her possessions. She was smiling because she had Marie in their greedy grip now and could easily manipulate her however she saw fit.

Robert had given his Pleasant View staff strict instructions on how Marie's care and medications should be administered. He was not aware that these instructions would be modified by Judy, later. He wanted her to feel comfortable, and ordered regular room service, where she could pick from the menu; a nurse was scheduled to check on Marie several times during the day. A physical therapist was ordered to work with her every day. The plan was to make Marie very comfortable so that she would feel welcomed, relaxed, and want to stay on at Pleasant View retirement center and make it her home. Robert really wanted his mother to stay where he could make sure she was safe.

Judy persuaded Robert they needed to advertise with a picture of his mother on their pamphlets showing the President and CEO's mother as a happy resident. Robert suggested awake and smiling, and Judy laughed. So as soon as Marie woke up, and they got her looking her loveliest, they would snap her picture for the cover of the new pamphlet.

Marie was too dazed to worry about anything. Everything happened so fast. After she was in her apartment for an hour, a nurse came in and asked her many of the same questions they had asked earlier, did she have a headache, or did she experience dizziness? Was she feeling nauseated, which could be the result of the concussion? Marie was so drugged up; she didn't feel anything and told them as much. She just needed to sleep she told them. Her every word went in her urgent care records. Dr. Allen prescribed more pain pills for her ankle and foot pain then gave her samples distributed by pharmaceutical representatives from a carton he kept in his office. He handed Marie several sample packs and watched her take the pill the nurse handed her with a small plastic cup of water.

Marie was so drugged already that she totally forgot all about her years of resistance to pharmaceuticals and readily took the pills they offered her. Frankly, at that point, she didn't care what they did to her or where they had wheeled her. She was very relaxed, feeling high and cheerful. She laughed and joked with the nurses. Seeing that she was a little out of it, Judy had the doctor add "delusional and absent-minded" to Marie's medical records. Marie blended right in with the other residents at Pleasant Valley who were sedated and manipulated by medications to relax them into calm compliancy. And of course, to add to their tallies of extra costs to be deducted from their lump sum savings accounts managed by Pleasant View.

CHAPTER TWELVE

The staff closely watched Marie's progress. They visited her apartment every four hours to administer more medications for pain and to keep Marie sedated. Marie easily got into the daily routine with meals and rehab as she wanted to get well. Marie was the most alert during physical therapy each afternoon.

The technicians and nurses were nice to her, but as time went on and the weeks passed, Marie was beginning to feel trapped and depressed. Even the sedatives and pain pills couldn't cover up the sickening feeling that Marie had that she was never going to leave Pleasant View. She soon realized that if she said anything negative about being there, she was given another pill. Marie caught on to this quickly and didn't complain about anything anymore but rather remained pleasant and pretended to be happy. Her best recall time occurred when sedative and pain pills were wearing off, right before they gave her more pills.

She hadn't seen Robert and Judy in weeks, it seemed. She thought, *they were probably trying to avoid her; afraid she would want to go home.* She hoped someone was looking after her house. She wanted to ask Robert, but he never returned her calls. She had a lot of time to think.

She remembered when Judy and Robert came to dinner at her house, how they had come on strong with their selling points regarding Pleasant View. Marie had resisted and now came to realize her resistance led them to resort to a more sinister plan to get her moved into Pleasant View. She wondered if Judy had really purposely spilled water on the floor. If so, the plan worked, they had her in their grip now. She could not really believe Robert would stoop that low, but she was here after all.

Marie sat quietly in her apartment in the wingback chair and stared out the window watching residents walk the path around the lake. In the distance she could see the Santa Rita and Catalina mountains. It was a peaceful and lovely sight.

She sat with her foot propped up on a little stool the nurse brought for her. She was not in pain; rather quite the opposite, she felt woozy and foggy.

The pain pills that Dr. Allen had prescribed for her in urgent care were automatically refilled and delivered to her apartment. Her meals were special made to order and delivered and would be until she was physically able to join other residents in the restaurant dining room.

As the weeks went on, Marie began to feel numb most of the time. She was in a daze and nothing seemed to matter anymore. She couldn't seem to think.

Marie didn't know that Robert and Judy were going through all her things at her house. Judy had told Robert it was the best thing they could do for his mother as she would not be able to do it now. She would appreciate them taking care of all that sorting and moving. They were looking through her prized possessions, her jewelry and antiques, things Frank had gotten for her, for their anniversaries and other special occasions. Robert and Judy worked for two months selling Marie's things and getting the house ready to put on the market.

Robert had already rolled over Marie's investments to Marie's Pleasant View account. Robert of course, planned to use his mother's money to build a second senior living facility. He was her son after all and the sole beneficiary; he could do what he wanted, so he figured. Why wait until she passed to use her money for future developments, use it now, she didn't need it.

Residents handed over their investment portfolios to Robert and Judy to manage it for them. Portfolio records and files were set up, but the money went directly into a Robert and Judy's Swiss bank accounts. If any resident wanted to see their monetary balance, they would see their full portfolio, the manipulated one. Judy figured a resident stay would probably be three to five years, then they would get sick and die, and Judy would report to family members that their loved one's money was all used up on living expenses, medicines, treatments at urgent care and other expenses. Judy easily produced a fictitious list of charges that she tallied every month, complete with dollar amounts, dates and statement detailing money deleted from their monetary accounts. Most accounts then had only enough money left in them for families to pay for funeral expenses.

CHAPTER THIRTEEN

Marie was bound and determined not to be taken down by Robert and Judy. In between doses, when the medicines began to wear off and Marie could think more clearly, she made mental notes to remind herself to pretend to take the pills that the nurse handed her. When the nurse came with her pills, Marie would take them from her and act like she swallowed them, but kept them in her hand. When the nurse wasn't looking, she slipped the pills into her pocket. She was so tired of feeling doped up; she just wanted a clear head. She repeatedly told the nurse that she was feeling better, until the nurse, although reluctant to go against what was prescribed, eased up a bit on the strength and number of medicines for Marie.

Feeling more alert, Marie spent more time out of her room, out of the wheelchair and using her crutches. Soon she began to join some of the other residents in the restaurant for dinner. She was grateful and happy to meet some of the other ladies.

"Hi, my name is Grace," smiled the eighty-year-old pleasant lady. She wore big round-framed glasses that matched the purple flower pattern in her dress. "Do you mind if I join you?" Grace asked, placing her hand on the back of the chair and pulled it out as Marie smiled and nodded.

"Yes, please do," Marie smiled, "I would love some company."

"I don't believe I have seen you here before. Are you new here?" Grace asked Marie as she sat down. Grace laid the folded newspaper she carried under her arm onto the table along with her reading glasses. She let out a sigh as she sat down, as if she was a much heavier woman instead of the thin, slight little lady she was.

"Well, I've been here for several months, just was having a rough time getting around since I injured my ankle," Marie replied. "This is my first visit to the dining room, I've been having my meals delivered."

"Well, I'm glad your ankle is better and that you are now able to get out and about." Grace smiled as she pushed her bangs to the side so she could see better as she picked up the menu. Marie thought the attractive woman sitting across from her had lovely hair. It was the color of golden wheat.

"You have such pretty hair," complimented Marie as she watched the woman sitting across from her. Marie hadn't had much contact with anyone except for the nurse, so having a clearer head and meeting a new friend was like the world opening for her.

"Oh, the beauty salon here has excellent hairdressers. I need to make an appointment, my bangs are getting too long," giggled Grace pushing them to the side again.

"Well, I certainly could use a trim myself," commented Marie, "my hair has gotten so long."

"Shall I make an appointment for you when I make my appointment?" Grace offered.

"Oh, that would be wonderful," Marie responded.

"I'm hungry, but I can't decide what I want to eat," Grace said as she looked over the menu. When the waitress finally appeared at their table they had both decided and were ready to order.

"Think I'll just have soup today," smiled Grace. "I'll have the vegetable beef soup."

"And I'll have the chicken rice soup," Marie said as she handed her menu back to the waitress.

"It's so nice to meet you, Grace. How long have you lived here?" Marie asked Grace as they settled back in their chairs, anticipating delicious soups to fill their hungry stomachs.

"Oh, I've been here over a year already, ever since the place opened. I was one of the first to sign up. I like it well enough." She smiled then went on, "My daughter and son-in-law are happy to have me here. Grace almost added, *and out of the way*, but decided not to. She was enjoying a pleasant meal with a new friend. "They were worried about me living alone after my husband died several years ago."

"Same here," agreed Marie, "I guess that is a pretty common story as to how we all came to move to Pleasant View."

Grace and Marie talked in detail about how each had first rejected the notion of moving into a retirement community that also had assistant living, memory care and nursing home facilities. They both laughed and agreed it was more like one stop shopping; once you were there you never really had to go anywhere else.

"I can't believe they never thought of building a funeral home and mortuary on the property," laughed Grace. "I realize that was pretty morbid," and laughed again.

"Yes, that would certainly be a full service then, wouldn't it?" Marie said and they both laughed.

Marie was curious about how Grace paid for Pleasant View and so casually brought it up over apple pie and coffee, after they finished their soup.

"Oh, I went with Pleasant View's suggested portfolio managing and paying plan and turned all my monetary assets over to Pleasant View, which gives you a discount then on the monthly fees," Grace said and then asked Marie what plan she chose.

"Well, my son is the head of Pleasant View and my financial and health power of attorney, so he will manage my affairs when the time comes," offered Marie. "I'm planning on returning home after my ankle heals and I am finished with physical therapy."

"I am hoping that I did the right thing," Grace said, looking concerned.

"Oh I'm sure you will be fine," remarked Marie even though she felt a little dubious herself about Robert and Judy managing other people's money.

"Well, I guess I can't go wrong then, if he has his own mother staying here."

"I am right here, but I sure don't see him much," said Marie.

"Well, I guess this place keeps him pretty busy. It's always filled to capacity, so I hear."

"Yes, so I'm sure it does keep him very busy," said Marie feeling a little sad at that moment and neglected by her son, and wondering how things were at her house. Being so heavily medicated she hadn't thought of it much, but now that her head was clearer she was beginning to want to go home.

Marie got to thinking that Pleasant View must be okay and must be doing all right, if there is a waiting list. She noticed the place was certainly filled with residents. The dining room was busy, and she saw residents sitting outside on the patio and walking the path that encircled the grounds.

"Well, here I am, good a place as any, I guess," sighed Grace.

As they sat resting their full stomachs, Grace got up to go the restroom. While Grace was away, Marie decided to look at the newspaper lying on the table that Grace had brought with her. She hadn't seen a paper in so long, so she read every line of every article. Everything seemed interesting to her, from headlines about the Reagan administration, crimes in the area, to even sports and real estate sales. She looked through everything as Grace stopped and talked to another resident on her way back to the table.

Suddenly a bold "sold" stamped over a "for sale" sign on a picture of a house caught her eye. It was her house! She blinked her eyes and looked again. She couldn't believe it. She read the address, yes; it was her house, all right. She was in shock. Robert and Judy had promised her that they would take care of everything while she was incapacitated with her ankle. But, she never dreamed that they would sell everything out from under her. She realized then that her promised "rehabilitation stay" at Pleasant View was never meant to be temporary, but meant to be permanent. *How could they do this to me?* She wondered what they did with all of her stuff. Nothing was ever mentioned to her about selling her house. In fact, she had not seen Robert or Judy in weeks. She had just a few things Judy brought when she arrived at Pleasant View.

"Is everything all right?" Grace asked when she sat down again. "You are looking a little pale." Marie was stunned and had not even noticed that Grace had returned to the table.

"I feel rather weak." Marie felt as if she were in shock. How dare they sell her things behind her back? Oh yeah, they took care of everything all right! Robert was her power of attorney; she suddenly figured that she was doomed. She had Robert's name on everything, even her car. She figured he probably sold that too, if he sold her house. She never dreamed he would do something like that without consulting her and getting her approval first. She felt hopeless and figured Robert had the nurses and doctors render her mentally unfit and incapable of making decisions. She was furious!

"Come on, I'll walk you back to your apartment," offered Grace as she could see that Marie was obviously shaken. "Is there something I can help you with?" asked Grace as they got off the elevator and walked down the hall to Marie's apartment.

"Would you like to come in for a cup of coffee?" Marie asked.

"Sure." Grace realized Marie had a lot of her mind and wanted to talk.

Grace sat on a stool at the snack bar while Marie scooped coffee into the coffee maker. She waited patiently to hear what was on Marie's mind. Something was plainly troubling her.

"Let's sit in the living room, shall we?" offered Marie as she handed Grace a cup of coffee. Grace added cream and sugar as Marie brought over the plate of cookies and set it on the coffee table.

"I just learned some disturbing news," Marie said as she sat down across from Grace.

"Oh, I'm so sorry to hear that," Grace said quietly in sympathy, "please go on."

"I had to read it in the newspaper of all things," Marie's voice cracked with emotion, "my son sold my house right out from under me." Marie was near tears.

"What?" Grace was astonished, "without you

knowing?" Grace couldn't believe what she was hearing.

"Well, Robert is my financial and healthcare power of attorney. But I had no idea when Robert said he would take care of everything that he would sell everything. I was planning on going back home!" Marie was most disturbed. *How rude, that Judy, I bet she talked him into selling everything*, she thought.

"Guess I should have expected this," Marie went on, "Robert's wife, 'Greedy Judy' I call her behind her back, has been after me to sell my house and to move in here. My falling and fracturing my ankle gave them ample opportunity to get me out of the way, to sell everything I own." Marie said reaching for a tissue.

"That's awful." Grace was sympathetic. Grace's situation was different because it was her idea. She was ready to move into senior living. She liked not having any responsibilities, which she wasn't going to bring up now, but rather just let Marie have her time to vent.

"Seems there comes a time when the kids just take over and make all the decisions," Grace mused.

"It's as if all my freedom has been taken away," Marie wiped her eyes, "I'm stuck here. I'm sure my car has been sold too." Marie was near tears.

"I know it's tough, you should not have had to find out by seeing your house for sale in a newspaper!" Grace was being very sympathetic.

"I have the hardest time trying to get an outside line to call anyone," Marie said.

"Oh, I have that problem too and their shuttle never

runs half the time either—everyone complains about that," Grace could certainly sympathize. "What are you going to do?"

"There isn't much that I can do," said Marie wiping her eyes. "I guess this is my home now."

After a while, Grace got up to leave. She gave Marie a hug when Marie walked her to the door.

"I really enjoyed your company," Marie said, "thanks for asking to join me for dinner."

"Oh, my pleasure, how about tomorrow then, same place, same time?"

Marie smiled she knew Grace was trying to make light of the whole nasty situation. "Sure, same place same time."

"I'll come by and knock on your door," suggested Grace.

They were happy to see that their living quarters were on the same floor right down the hall from each other. Marie didn't like her situation, but at least she made a new friend.

CHAPTER FOURTEEN

Several weeks went by, Marie was feeling much better, and she didn't need to use the crutches any longer and switched to using a cane. Of course, she still had to wear the silly boot cast, but she managed okay when she and Grace would go for short strolls in the garden. Marie promised Grace that soon her ankle would be as good as new and then she could walk faster. Grace didn't really mind having to walk slower for Marie. She enjoyed Marie's company and their conversations about Pleasant View, the food, gossip about the staff and residents. There was never a lull in the conversation.

"That lady down the hall from me, Joan," Grace said sounding very concerned, "died last night. You remember her, Marie, don't you?" Grace went on to describe her, "small, thin, Asian, had short silver hair, wore black rimmed glasses. She sat with us at dinner a couple of times, remember?"

"I remember Joan, sure," stated Marie looking over at Grace as they walked through the garden and nodded greetings at the other residents as they passed by. It was a beautiful day in the desert, there was a gentle breeze and the birds were singing. Marie had practically forgotten about losing her house, she didn't care anymore—it wasn't that bad here.

Having Grace as a friend helped a lot. She felt older though and guessed it was probably part of the aging process realizing she was in her last chapters of her life. She was at peace with death because she believed in the afterlife and reincarnation. Someone once told her, you can plan your passing. You can plan it as a quick painless transition back to the source, where loved ones will greet you. She wondered what Joan's beliefs were, and hoped that she was in a good place.

"So sorry to hear about Joan," Marie sympathized, "I didn't realize that she was ill."

"Far as I know, she wasn't ill," said Grace. "but she was on a lot of medications. She said she didn't understand why; mostly, for prevention, she guessed."

"Makes me wonder," Marie couldn't believe what she was hearing. Right away Marie's want-to-be investigative reporter mind went to thoughts about Joan's spending account and wondered if her money was running low. The plan at Pleasant View was that if you had moved in with at least three hundred thousand dollars, you were assured a home for life. Even if you went through all of your money, you could stay on without charge and you would not have to worry about having to pay the three thousand dollars per month fee. It's why Pleasant View was so poplar and had a long waiting list, seniors like the idea of being guaranteed a home for as long as they lived. *Was it too good to be true?* Marie wondered as she and Grace chatted.

"Joan appeared perfectly healthy, active and seemed happy," said Grace and added, "Anyway, she never complained of anything."

"Have you heard why she died?" asked Marie.

"Some of the other residents heard that it was a stroke," suggested Grace.

"My, how tragic," noted Marie sympathetically.

"Joan had told me several times that she never had high blood pressure or high cholesterol and that she wanted to get off all those 'preventive' medicines they had her on. Joan also told me that she felt that if you lived at Pleasant View, the management expected you to be on all the medicines.

"Do you take that many?" asked Marie.

"I was taking at least ten different medicines and had no idea what they were for and most of them were expensive. We know all too well don't we, having expensive medicines… They won't let you not take them, so I fake take them."

"So do I," admitted Marie.

"I think we should go to the funeral home."

"I think that's a good idea."

CHAPTER FIFTEEN

Grace and Marie made arrangements to take the Pleasant View shuttle to the funeral home located several blocks away. There they paid their respects to Joan's family who were sad and grieving over Joan's apparent untimely demise. Joan's son, Joe, was shocked that Pleasant View had gone through Joan's money, all three hundred fifty thousand dollars of it, in just under two years. When he learned Grace and Marie were friends from Pleasant View, he shared his concerns with them.

"Yes, when we went to settle up with Pleasant View and to get Mom's remaining money," complained Joe, "there was only about fifteen thousand left, just enough to settle remaining medical bills that hadn't been deducted yet and to bury her."

"Oh my, that's too bad," Marie was sympathetic but felt a sudden dreadful reminder of her own her situation. She was still upset with how Robert and

Judy confiscated her house, her money, and all of her possessions.

"I don't know the reason for all the pills," said Joe. "I suppose preventive."

"Yes, seems they believe in using a lot of preventive medicines," added Grace.

"Yes, Mom always complained about all the meds she had to take," said Joe leaning his tall lanky body against the door jamb when he didn't see an available chair to sit on. He suddenly felt old and tired.

"We loved your mother's company, and we'll miss her," said Grace with tears in her eyes. She cocked her head and looked up at Joe inquisitively then, feeling he had more to share.

"She complained that the food always had an odd taste," noted Joe standing up straight now. "She wondered if it was the seasoning or if it was a side effect to her taste buds from taking all those medications." Joe's eyebrows rose inquisitively "Have you ladies noticed anything like that?"

"No, but now that you mentioned it. What about you Marie?" Grace turned to Marie. "What do you think? Have you noticed a difference in taste and smell?"

"Well my stomach did get upset the other day," Marie rubbed her stomach recalling that she had bad cramps then. It was the day Grace walked with her back to her apartment and came in for a while because Marie felt unsteady, and of course she had just received bad news. Of course, she felt sick, it was the day that she saw the "sold" sign splattered across the for-sale picture of her house in the newspaper. *Getting news that your house was sold out from under you would upset anyone,* Marie thought.

CHAPTER SIXTEEN

The next day, Marie met with Grace, and other resident friends, Alice and Margaret, for their morning walk. As they walked through the halls, they saw someone moving into Joan's old apartment.

"Hello," Grace introduced herself to the new tenant who was being helped by her son, daughter-in-law and two kids.

"Oh Hi, my name is Betty, and this is my family," said Betty as she introduced them.

The ladies introduced themselves and invited Betty to join them for dinner in the dining room that evening, then continued on their way outside for their walk around the grounds, where they chatted about the quick turnaround of Joan's apartment.

"Well it certainly did not take long to fill Joan's apartment vacancy," remarked Grace with a frown, "now did it?" She wished it could have been left uninhabited for a while in memorial to Joan.

"Long waiting list, remember," said Marie as she quickened her step and led the ladies outdoors. Marie was all smiles because her ankle felt so much better and she did not have to wear that cumbersome support boot.

"Marie, so glad you don't have to wear that nasty boot anymore," offered Grace. Alice and Margaret had to agree too, for each of them also had their experiences with sprains and fractures. They each proceeded to share their stories of when they had to wear one of those boots. Alice once had a sprained ankle and Margaret had suffered a fractured toe.

"I am so glad. It was so tough to walk wearing it, because none of my shoes matched the boot's height so I was always limping," Marie said and the ladies all agreed. They walked and chatted and enjoyed an extra-long trek around the paved path that surrounded the lake and grounds. The birds were feeding and singing at the feeders. The ladies enjoyed their songs, along with fragrant colorful roses, mixed with the smell of freshly mowed grass. The grounds were kept green and fresh as a small desert oasis. The ladies enjoyed their walk and afterwards each retreated to their own apartments for a long afternoon nap before they would regroup again for dinner.

Betty showed up promptly at four-thirty in the dining hall and sat with Marie, Grace, Alice and Margaret at a round table in the corner.

"So, Betty have you gotten all settled in?" asked Grace.

"Oh, yes, it's a lovely little apartment. I almost have everything put away. I believe I have just enough room to put all my things so it doesn't look cluttered."

"Yes, they are small," commented Margaret who had stacks of clothes and books that she hated to part with and filled her apartment.

"Your family seems very nice," said Marie.

"Thank you," said Betty. "Yes, the family is growing. My kids wanted my big house for their expanding family."

"Yes, needs change," said Marie, again being reminded of her own situation and wanting to avoid questions about it, asked Betty another question. "Does your family live close by?"

"Oh, just a couple of hours away," responded Betty, "I'll miss them, of course, but they promised to come and visit often. I wish it wasn't so far away. My son picked this place because of its popular reputation. He was impressed by the article he read about it in the paper a while back."

The ladies lingered in the dining room, sipping coffee and enjoying chocolate cake for dessert. Betty got up first saying she wanted to put a few things away and then relax in her new apartment. With farewells of a pleasant evening, they promised to meet for breakfast in the dining room in the morning.

CHAPTER SEVENTEEN

Weeks passed; the days ran together after a while. The ladies spent their time walking the winding paths through palm trees, flowers, and cactus plants. Most days the weather was lovely and they enjoyed lunch on the patio under umbrella tables. There they met other residents and played trivia and other group games. During those times, with friends, Marie had practically forgotten everything about her old life. There was really only one person that she missed and that was her friend Ann who lived in Sedona. Marie missed traveling to Sedona to visit her good friend. She wondered if Ann was worried about her. Under all the medications, Marie's mind was foggy, and she couldn't even remember Ann's phone number or where she had put it.

CHAPTER EIGHTEEN

Ann had been trying to reach her good friend, Marie, for weeks. It was so unlike Marie not to contact her or send her a card for her birthday. Ann tried to call Robert and Judy. She left several messages but never received a return call. Ann was concerned because when she had tried to call Marie's house she got an automated message stating that the phone had been disconnected and no longer in service.

Finally, Ann decided to drive the four hours from Sedona to Tucson to check on Marie. When she drove up to Marie's house, she realized the place did not look the same. It didn't look neat and tidy the way Marie always kept it. The walks needed sweeping, the windows were dirty, and the lawn was over grown and needed mowing. She had an eerie feeling when she walked up to the front door and knocked. Something did not feel right. After several knocks on the door, she was about to turn and leave when the door opened, and a young stranger greeted her with an inquisitive look on her face.

"Hello, can I help you?" the woman asked pulling her long hair from her eyes as she opened the storm door just so far.

"I was looking for Marie. Is she home?" asked an astonished Ann.

There is no one here by that name," explained the friendly young woman, she looked at Ann rather strangely thinking maybe Ann had come to the wrong house on the wrong street. After all, the houses pretty much all looked the same in the subdivision.

"Oh, I am sorry, I guess my friend moved then," Ann said with a shaky voice realizing that Marie was indeed gone. She feared that she might never see her dear friend again. It was indeed a strange feeling to walk up to a familiar door, expect to see your friend open the door, and a complete stranger appears.

"We just moved in," explained the young woman, "who did you say you were looking for?"

"Her name is Marie, Marie Dems," said Ann in total shock. "Oh, my, I had no idea, she moved," confessed Ann "I am so sorry to have intruded on your day," Then as she began to turn away she thought to ask.

"I don't suppose you know where the former resident moved to, do you by chance?" asked Ann with a hopeful tone.

"No, I am so sorry, but I don't." The woman looked concerned then went on, "Did you say Dems? We recently bought the house," explained the woman, "from a Mr. Robert Dems."

"Oh you did. Well, thank you for your help," Ann said as she turned to walk down the sidewalk to her car parked in the street. She decided to check into a motel for the night. She was just too troubled and weary to go on and search for her friend; besides, she had no idea where she might be. The discovery that Marie had moved without telling her, drained her energy. Ann had to take time to process just what was going on. She checked in at a hotel after picking up something to eat. She needed to relax and she needed to think—and to shift her FBI investigative mind back into gear. She was determined to find Marie.

Ann decided to do a little investigating and checked government records and she found no record of death certificate for Marie. So she knew Marie was still alive. She checked with the hospitals and found no records of her admission into any nearby facilities. She checked the sale of Marie's house, and the title company records showed a Robert Dems signed the closing papers as Marie's financial power of attorney. Did Marie have a stroke? Was she incapable of making her own decisions? Was she staying with Robert and Judy? A thousand questions went through Ann's mind.

Ann was worried and saddened at the thought of her dear friend being incapacitated. Ann thought of her dear friend's visits to Sedona, and all the fun they had attending psychic readings and metaphysical lectures, visiting the Grand Canyon and hiking the many trails surrounding the red rocks in the Sedona area. She knew Marie loved Sedona as much as she did. Whatever happened to Marie, must have happened suddenly; because surely Marie would have called and told her if something was going on with her health. Ann was determined to find out what happened to her friend.

CHAPTER NINETEEN

"Marie, are you in there?" Grace knocked feverishly at Marie's apartment door. The neighbors heard her so surely Marie could hear her. She wondered why Marie didn't answer. Margaret joined her then, and then Betty came from her apartment. They were gathering for their morning walk. Marie didn't show up for breakfast in the dining room, but then sometimes Marie skipped breakfast.

Grace was concerned, because it seemed as of late, that Marie was more distant, and more into her own thoughts. Grace was afraid Marie was depressed about her son and all, and the fact that her son who even owned the place never came to check on her. Grace knew Marie was still taking a boatload of pills every day, even though she tried to hide some and not take them. They pushed a lot of pills on everyone, but more onto Marie than what normally was given to the other residents.

Finally, after moments of Grace's persistent knocking, Marie slowly opened the door a ways and peered out. She looked around at the ladies with a puzzled look on her face until she figured out why the ladies were standing at her door looking at their watches and telling her it was mid-morning already.

"Oh my gosh," explained Marie in a low sedated voice, "I just woke up."

"Wow you must have really been out of it," said Grace when she saw how dazed Marie looked.

"Yes, I guess I was," Marie said slowly, sounding as if she couldn't believe it herself. She saw the ladies look at each other as if to say—shall we be worried about her. But she didn't care what they thought.

"Are you walking with us today?" Margaret asked.

"Yes, of course." Marie moved so the ladies could enter. "Come in while I get my shoes on. I'll just be a minute."

The ladies followed her inside. The ladies walked into what smelled like a pharmaceutical dispensary and looked like one too. There were pill bottles everywhere on her kitchen sink and pills in a couple of plastic cases with the days of the week stamped on each little compartment.

Marie realized she was moving rather slowly but for some reason she didn't care—she was in the zone, a very relaxed zone. They walked slowly that morning so Marie could keep up. They were concerned; Marie had been doing so well and now had seemed to relapse. They offered to shorten the route, but Marie insisted that they walk their normal course.

After their walk they ordered lunch on the patio. Everyone had a hardy appetite after the morning walk, but Marie mostly pushed around the salad on her plate and ate only half of her slice of pizza. She didn't have much to say, and it wasn't long before she got up and announced that she was going back to her apartment to take a nap. Grace, Margaret and Betty remained behind sitting in the shade under the umbrella table. They were concerned and discussed Marie's condition.

"You know this place does hand out a lot of pills," reported Betty, and Margaret and Grace agreed.

"Yes, ever since I have moved in, I have taken dozens of pills: A pill for this, a pill for that, and it goes on and on. And we are expected to get health exams every month too; which to me, is just another way to fake find something and give them an excuse to prescribed us even more pills.

"And you know that costs money," complained Margaret, "I know my savings account here has gone way down just within a couple of years—how can that be?"

"I know, I try to refuse all the pills," added Betty, "but they tell me, oh so and so is sick with this and that and you don't want to catch it, so take this pill, and take that pill, it seems there is no end to it."

"Yes, they certainly are ready with the pills aren't they," frowned Grace.

"Well, I feel fine," commented Betty, "so I guess maybe they are looking out for us. She did not want to think that any wrongdoing was taking place.

"I guess, they don't want any bad publicity of having a senior living center filled with sick people," added Margaret.

"I don't know about the food here, though," said Betty, "I just can't get used to the seasoning or whatever it is they do to the food every day," she complained. "I realize that I am acting like a crabby old lady. Maybe one day I'll get used to the way they cook things around here."

"My gosh, what's going on?" Margaret asked as she turned and saw the ambulance pull up near the medical center around the corner. They got up and moved closer and watched as a gurney was being rolled out of the ambulance and into the south entrance of the building. Within a few minutes, they noticed that someone was lying on it, covered up, as ambulance attendants rolled the gurney back to the ambulance. Betty went ahead to get a closer look on what was going and walked over to join a group of residents standing near the ambulance. She came back and reported what a resident had told her.

"Harry said it was Mr. Jones. He just collapsed, and Dr. Allen and the nurses couldn't wake him up." Harry, being a fairly new resident, then walked over to where Betty had joined the ladies to get better acquainted.

"Yeah, poor Mr. Jones, he's been here the longest," Harry explained, "he really hadn't been sick that much—he worried a lot though. He worried about his money running out." Harry went on, "I tried to tell him that even if they used up all his money on room and board and medical needs, that according to policy, after you run out and had been a resident for more than five years that they would keep you on, so not to worry. But Mr. Jones was a worrier. I always called him Mr. Jones out of respect—him being a college professor and all. I can't believe this happened to him."

"Was he ill?" asked Margaret sounding concerned.

"Mr. Jones was healthy has a horse," Harry said with conviction.

"Well, I'm sorry this happened to your friend," said Margaret, "I hate to hear news like that, him just dropping over dead, can you imagine?"

There was certain stillness around Pleasant View that evening as they gathered in the dining room for dinner. The residents realized that Mr. Jones was one of many they had seen carted out of Pleasant View in recent months. It was a sobering time, to realize that there were three in the past week alone that were carted out to ambulances.

There were about three hundred residents living in Pleasant View and to think that there could be more deaths in the coming weeks frightened everyone. Little did they want to suspect that perhaps wrongdoing was going on. It was out of their realm of thinking to even imagine that deliberate wrongdoing could be taking place at Pleasant View.

Little did the residents suspect that Judy and Dr. Allen contributed to the quick turnaround of residents. The current residents did not realize that there was a long waiting list of folks with lots of retirement money, waiting to move in. As soon as the rooms became available, seniors on the waiting list were notified that they had a vacancy and could move in. Mr. Jones had a significant amount of money left in his account. It really wasn't near depletion, as he feared; but Pleasant View's common fraudulent accounting practices depicted much lower amounts in resident's statements. Grieving family members never suspected any wrongdoing. To them it was reasonable that people naturally get old, sick and die. Death was just part of the natural course of life.

CHAPTER TWENTY

Weeks passed, and the ladies made it a point to walk every day. Marie, Grace, Alice, Betty and Margaret couldn't help but notice that they didn't see several of the regular walkers. Like all other mornings, they wanted to keep conversations light and spirits up. So no one said too much about not seeing some of the regular walkers they normally saw. Instead of discussing what was obviously on everyone's mind, they walked by the rose garden to see how the roses were fairing, after the rain they had received the night before.

All concerns were forgotten as they walked and listened to the birds, held and petted a visiting puppy, and engaged in idle chitchat with other residents. Watching the squirrels scurrying about and rummaging in every unattended trash bin entertained them. They looked up as a flock of birds flew overhead heading towards the palm trees that circled lake, an oasis in the middle of the desert that Pleasant View was fortunate to have to enjoy. They were happily engaged in the sight and sounds of nature until Margaret spoke up complaining about her stomach feeling icky.

"I'm going to have to stop at the restroom," complained Margaret as they walked," She quickly picked up her pace.

"Oh my, what's going on?" asked Alice as Margaret jogged towards the main building.

"Sorry ladies, it must have been something I ate for breakfast, Margaret's voice trailed off as she hurried towards the center's recreation area where restrooms were located.

"We'll wait for you," shouted Grace realizing it was a common problem they shared. Margaret waved an acknowledgement without turning around as she picked up the pace and hoped the restroom would not be busy. She didn't think she could wait one minute longer. Much to her relief, she made it in time. Her stomach was cramping and she made a mental note to get someone in management to speak to the new chef.

Several months had passed and the ladies were still having problems with their stomachs after they ate the food that was served in the main dining room. The ladies had noticed stomach problems ever since a new chef came on board. Shortly after he arrived a new menu was introduced. The ladies were a little worried about the smell and taste of the food, but figured they would grow accustomed to the new seasoning or whatever the chef used in his recipes. The food wasn't quite up to par, but at the same time, they noticed, too, that fewer pills were being handed out, and for that they were grateful.

Still, the ladies were worried, because the food smelled and tasted funny. They pondered the thought that maybe instead of nurses handing out medicines; that the cooks were putting the medicines directly into the food? Could that even be possible? They wondered how dosages would be controlled? The main restaurant in the living center was their only source of daily meals, unless they ordered food to be delivered from an outside restaurant, and of course that was frowned upon.

And most times when an order was placed to an outside restaurant for delivery, it never showed up. Margaret was afraid that deliveries were being intercepted at the guard's desk, and those deliveries ended up as lunch or dinner for the guards to eat or take home to their families. The ladies were nervous but still joked about conspiracy theories. Margaret didn't think their joking was funny, as she was becoming more concerned about her health, because she was not feeling well at all.

"Come on Margaret, let's go for our morning walk," Grace hollered through the locked door. She knocked and knocked. Finally, Margaret opened her door and Grace's sentence trailed off into silence and her eyes grew large in astonishment. Poor Margaret looked awful and she could barely speak above a whisper.

"I'm not feeling so well this morning," she said leaning against the door frame, too weak to stand up straight.

"Oh my! You need to sit down," ordered Grace, seeing how frail Margaret looked. She led Margaret back inside.

"You ladies better go on without me, this morning." Margaret said.

Grace closed the door and helped Margaret get to the nearest chair. Margaret flopped into the chair and sat with her arm resting on the chair arms, her hand holding her head up; her other hand clutching her stomach. She was so thin and pale. Grace did not know what to do. She quickly got Margaret some lemon-lime soda she found in the refrigerator. She hoped the sweet soda would settle Margaret's stomach a bit. Margaret thanked her as she took the small glass from her and slowly sipped the soothing liquid. After she drank it all she sat the glass down next to her on the lamp table and sat staring at Grace.

Her eyes were red and glassy looking. Grace was frightened to the point where she was shaking as she sat down on the sofa across from her. Then in an earth shattering silence, Margaret's eyes closed and her head slumped down to her chest. Grace hoped Margaret had fallen asleep, but in her heart she knew that Margaret had passed over into the spiritual plane. She was gone.

Grace was sickened and shaken to the core as she pressed the red emergency button located in the apartment near the door. In seconds the nurse was there, knocking twice on the door then using their special key to unlock the door and let herself in. Grace couldn't move from the sofa and only pointed in Margaret's direction as the nurse came rushing in. The nurse urgently felt for a pulse in the thick blue veins around Margaret neck and in her thin wrist, there was none.

Marie, Grace, Alice and Betty were also losing weight. They thought it was their daily walks keeping them fit and trim or at least that is what they hoped. Marie had already missed several morning walks complaining she wasn't feeling well. They were all worried. The ladies had noticed in recent months more ambulances coming and taking residents to the nearby hospital — or maybe to the morgue because many never returned.

They were becoming more concerned and weren't sure about anything anymore. One thing that they were sure of was the large turnover in residents within the last several months.

CHAPTER TWENTY-ONE

Grace was feeling pretty energetic and decided to go for another walk by herself before lunch. As she was leaving the south entrance, she began to chat with the new guard, who introduced himself as Ed. He was chewing, as he talked and Grace smelled a faint but rather delicious aroma coming from behind the desk where he stood. Ed smiled at her.

"You caught me," he said softly, "don't tell anyone." He grinned.

"That's not from the restaurant here is it?" Grace said with a smile. She could tell a distinct aroma from what Ed was eating, and knew it was not from the restaurant.   Ed shook his head no.

"Sure smells good," commented Grace. It smelled so good her stomach was growling.

"It's from the new deli down the street," Ed said with his mouth full, trying to hurry and eat his lunch before he got caught by management.

"Well it sure smells good."

"The sandwiches and soups are so delicious," Ed said as he wiped his mouth with a napkin. He looked at Grace and saw how sad she looked, and it made his heart ache, so he offered to get deli food for her.

"How about I get a sandwich and some soup for you," offered Ed feeling bad that he was eating in front of her. He thought she was a sorry sight, the way her dress just hung on her, as if it were hanging on a clothes hanger.

Grace wasn't really that thin. Ed was just such a big guy that everyone looked little and too thin to him.

"Oh, I wouldn't want to put you out." Grace was practically drooling. She couldn't take her eyes off his sandwich and soup, and Ed certainly noticed.

"How about I get you something from the deli while I'm on break," Ed repeated his offer.

"Oh my, that would be wonderful." Normally Grace would refuse, but today she eagerly agreed. The delicious smelling aromas that drifted up from Frank's sandwich and soup as she watched him devour both had hypnotized her.

"Anything else I can get you?" offered Ed.

"Why yes, how about getting the same soup and sandwich for my friend Marie."

"You got it, young lady," Ed smiled. It warmed his heart to hear Grace think of her friend, too, not just herself. Grace went for a walk and when she returned to the guard's desk, he handed her the plain brown paper bag filled with two orders of soup and sandwiches. Grace whispered thanks, and quickly took the stairs up to Marie's apartment to share the goodies with her.

Grace had told Ed how weak Marie was and Ed promised to get food for Grace and her friend Marie every day. He only offered to do it for those two ladies, because he was afraid of getting caught and maybe losing his job. It took him forever to find this security guard job and he didn't want to jeopardize it. He knew the managers wanted everyone to eat food from the restaurant. Ed smiled when Grace took an oath, crossed her heart and hoped to die, if she told another soul.

***

Grace couldn't wait to get to Marie's apartment to share lunch with her. She only had to knock twice before Marie appeared at the door. Grace was glad to see that at least Marie was up and about and moving.

"I brought us lunch," whispered Grace, "I think you are going to like this."

Marie asked no questions, and quickly grabbed some spoons and napkins then sat at the table, while Grace filled glasses of water then got the sandwiches and soup containers out and opened them up. The delicious aroma filled the apartment and Marie perked up in her chair ready to dig in.

"Here's yours," smiled Grace as she placed a sandwich and container of soup in front of Marie. Marie had become quit consumed with grief after Grace broke the news to her of Margaret's passing, so having a treat for Marie made her feel good.

"Sure smells good," whispered Marie ready to dig in.

"This will be good for you," ordered Grace, "you need to build your strength."

"Oh, this soup is delicious." Marie sat up straight as she dipped into the thick vegetable beef soup and ate her sandwich. Grace could tell Marie was beginning to feel better with each bite and spoonful.

"This is so good."

"I had it smuggled in," Grace whispered with a smile.

"What?" Marie managed between bites.

"I've gotten cozy with, Ed, the new guard. He works downstairs in the lobby at the south side entrance. I stopped and chatted with him leaving for a walk a while ago. We chatted and I caught him sneaking bites of food while we talked. We got to talking about the food the restaurant here served, and how the taste had changed. He said he thought that I looked too thin. I said I didn't like the food here. He had just taken the last big bite of his sandwich and bragged about how good the food was from the new deli down the street and offered to get us some."

"Such a kind man," Marie murmured as she sipped her soup.

"And he's going to get us lunch every day, isn't that wonderful!" Grace exclaimed.

"Oh my, that's so kind of him," Marie responded after finishing the sandwich and spooning out the last little bit of soup that was left in the bottom of the bowl.

Marie smiled, and her eyes lit up after she finished eating and wiped her mouth with her napkin. It was the first time in a long time that Grace saw Marie smile. The sad news about Margaret's passing had only deepened Marie's woes. It seemed the tasty food helped to brighten her spirits. Grace sat with her for a while after they ate; they chatted about this and that. When Grace saw Marie doze off, she said a quick good-bye and slipped out the door to join Betty and Alice for a walk outside, so they could talk in private.

Lately, Grace had grown suspicious of cameras and microphones in hallways. She didn't trust anyone anymore. Was she becoming paranoid and senile in her old age, she wondered. She knew she had to be careful of conversations being overheard. She was afraid that she and her friends could end up in the lost memory wing, and under heavy sedation to keep them quiet and out of the way.

"Betty, how have you been feeling?" Grace asked as they slowly walked and found a vacant bench on the patio where the three could sit for moment. Grace tried to act as casual as she could to not upset Betty. But Grace and Alice both noticed that Betty's color was not as good as it once was, and she looked as if she had lost more weight.

"I feel as if we are all slipping away far too soon and far too fast," Betty said with a frown. "Something is not quite right here at Pleasant View."

"Yes, I agree," answered Grace, "what can we do—it does no good to complain to the managers. The owners never come around to listen to us share our concerns and no one else here in management seems to care."

"It's like we are prisoners here," Betty added, "even calls to my son are not getting through. He certainly isn't calling me back, and I haven't heard from him in a long time. And when I try to schedule a shuttle to take me to the train station so I can visit him, I am told that the shuttles are all booked up. Yet, I do not see any shuttles leaving or returning."

"I saw Mr. Jones' friend, Harry, as I was coming down the hallway and he looked very weak and pale," sighed Alice. "Maybe there's a virus going around."

The ladies visited for a bit, and then Grace and Alice helped Betty back to her apartment, before returning to theirs.

CHAPTER TWENTY-TWO

Ann sat on her patio in the warm Sedona sunshine sipping iced tea while enjoying the stunning view of surrounding red rocks. Her patio had a great view of Coffee Pot rock. She had just returned from hiking in Boynton Canyon, kicked off her hiking boots, and propped her feet up on a chair. *Marie should be here sitting in that chair*, she thought. All the while she hiked that morning, she thought of her friend Marie and wondered if she was still in Tucson. Ann had not heard from Marie in months. She had sent a letter but it was returned, stamped: party no longer at this address. Apparently, there was no forwarding address left at the post office for Marie.

Ann decided to contact her FBI friend, Pete. Pete had been her investigating partner at the bureau for years, and they always worked well together. Pete would have retired from the bureau when Ann retired, but with kids in college, he couldn't afford to so he was still working.

Pete was surprised and happy to hear from Ann when she called. They talked about old times and cases they had worked on together that were still unresolved. After they got caught up and the conversation had a low, Ann asked Pete if he would do a favor for her.

"Anything, for you Ann," Pete said. "What's going on?"

"Well, Pete, I have a missing friend," explained Ann. "Her name is Marie Dems. I would like you to search for her. I think a big clue may be her son. So, I would like you to check up on him, too. His name is Robert Dems. If you find him, you may find her."

"So what do you think is going on?"

"I think he has her somewhere, maybe in some kind of home, or maybe in his own home," Ann sounded worried and Pete picked up on it.

"Want me to run a check on him too then?"

"Yes, because I found that Marie's phone had been disconnected. So I drove to Tucson to check it out. When I knocked on the door, the woman who answered said she did not know Marie, but that she and her husband bought the house from a man named Robert Dems."

"I'll get right on it," Pete said, "and see what I can find."

"I am very worried," said Ann, "I know that Marie planned on living in her house for a long time. She loved her independence. She loved driving here to Sedona to visit me."

"Okay, don't worry, I've got this." Pete was eager to help; he had worked on many missing person cases throughout his career. He knew right where to start.

"Thanks Pete, you're the best!" Ann was grateful.

"I'll get back with you in a day or two," said Pete, "I should have something by then.

Pete promptly did as she asked and within three days got back in touch with her and reported on what he found.

"I found that Robert Dems was deep in debt, has filed extensions on loans and taxes he owes, and contractors have not been paid or are suing him. And yes, as you suspected, he did sign the papers for the sale of Marie's house and her car." Pete verified and went on, "Robert is indeed power of attorney and healthcare power of attorney for his mother, Marie Dems, location unknown at this time. But, Robert Dems and his wife Judy own a senior living center in Tucson called Pleasant View."

"That's great information, Pete," Ann exclaimed excited to get some answers to her questions, "and it gives me a lot to go on."

With Pete's help, Ann looked into Robert Dems' senior living community financial records and found nearly bankrupt conditions, which gave rise to Ann's worries about Marie's whereabouts. Ann knew Marie would not just up and move without letting her know. Ann's years of experience in criminal investigations led her to believe that Marie may have become a victim of foul play, so she stepped up her investigation—spending every hour of the day digging into files and records on Robert and Judy Dems. She found some disturbing things about Judy, too.

According to police records that Ann read, detectives

ruled Roger Blake's death as accidental under unproven suspicious circumstances. The brake line was cut but not a clean cut. The cut was jagged and frayed, which meant cut and torn to look like wear and tear caused by pressure or friction. Roger Blake died in a car crash, whether or not it was an accident was not able to be proven. Investigations showed that the brakes failed on the car he was driving as he drove down the mountain road that led from the house where he and Judy lived. It was evident that the brake line was torn or cut. But prosecutors felt there was not enough evidence to proceed with a criminal investigation, even though the timing of his death was suspicious, as Roger's lawyer had just served Judy with divorce papers shortly before the crash happened. Judy would get half of everything through a divorce. Ann had a suspicious criminal mind from working with the FBI for years, and thought, *Why would Judy want to get half of everything, when she could be a widow and get everything?*

Ann researched police records and found that at the time of Judy's first husband's death, the local police on the case had investigated but never came up with enough evidence to go after Judy. Records showed that the prosecutor never went after Judy because he said anything could have caused the ragged cut to the brake line.

Judy was all set up with more than enough money, she didn't really have to get a job, but Ann figured that Judy was bored and wanted to meet a man. She figured the best place for Judy to meet someone with money, was where money flows, like where she met her first husband, at an investment firm. So, she went to work at another investment banking firm and that was where she met an aspiring junior officer named Robert Dems.

Ann was intrigued by what she learned about Judy's past, and she feared Marie was in danger. She was determined to find her.

CHAPTER TWENTY-THREE

Marie was feeling a bit better and straightened up her apartment and prepared something to eat from left over's in the refrigerator. The dinners served in the dining room were all too large and she would end up with a refrigerator full of leftovers to eat. Marie sat on the couch eating from a TV tray and looking out the big window in her living room. She liked to watch visitors come and go in hopes that her son would be one of them. She was excited when she spotted a big red Cadillac pull up near the main entrance, hoping Robert was coming to visit.

"It's Robert!" Marie said out loud as she got up to move to the window to get a better look. She grimaced at the sound of her own rough gravelly voice; she'd been hoarse and feeling ill for weeks. Her body ached, but she managed to move closer to the window to get a better view. Yes, it was Robert and Judy who had pulled up in their big red shiny Cadillac convertible with the top down. There was no way she could have missed their grand entrance. She wondered how many times in the past that they had been there and had not come to her visit her. She felt that they avoided her on purpose.

So Robert was on the premises. She certainly wanted to talk to him, tell him the food was awful and she was tired of having to take so many pills. The pills obviously were not helping if she was becoming weak and frail. She was going to hurry down to the lobby and speak to Robert.

She had many questions for Robert; one being, where have you been? It had been months since Marie had seen him. She gathered all her strength and put her shoes on and hurried out of her apartment, down the hall to the elevators. She pushed the elevator button, stepped back and waited. When the elevator door opened, both Robert and Judy appeared before her. Their eyes grew big as they spotted Marie—although at first they were not sure it was Marie, she had lost so much weight and appeared drawn and thin. But she had the same unforgettable determined look in her eye.

"Mother!" Robert grimaced at the sight of her, "what are you doing up?" He couldn't believe how frail she looked. He headed her off like a border collie would block a wayward lamb that wandered away from the flock. Robert held his arms out, not to hug, but to steer her around the other way, back to her apartment.

"Robert!" muttered Marie in a dazed state of disbelief, "Is that you?" Marie asked, as she stood frozen in her tracks at the sight of him.

Robert quickly put his hands on her shoulders and swept his mother back to her apartment, practically shoving her inside as soon as she got the door unlocked. Judy rolled her eyes, as if disappointed, at seeing Marie was still alive. She could use this apartment if it were available for some new money to move in. Robert and Judy were seriously in a hurry and wanted to get her out of sight. They didn't want her out of her apartment thinking she may complain to other residents about how Judy and Robert stole her life by selling her house, her car and everything right out from under her, and sticking her in this place against her will. They couldn't have her leave. How would that look to potential interested seniors who wanted to take up residence there?

Judy rolled her eyes again as she chewed gum, slipped off her wide-brim hat, and fluffed her thick red curls. She was bored with all the questions, as Marie rattled them off.

"Just what is going on here, Robert?" Marie confronted her son as soon as he closed the apartment door.

"Mother sit down," Robert demanded. Marie totally ignored him and began to pace in front of Robert and Judy as they sat on the couch looking impatient and businesslike.

Judy looked smug as she sat there in her tailored white cashmere suit, which was a one-of-a-kind creation by her designer in Paris. She sat straight and tall and casually adjusted the white wide-brim hat that framed her big green eyes, made up with sage colored shadow to match her eyes. Robert unbuttoned the button on his expensive charcoal colored Armani suit jacket as he sat next to Judy on the couch. They sat like royalty, pretending to care about what Marie had to say.

"Robert, where have you been?" sighed Marie, "I haven't seen you in months."

"Mother! I was here last week," insisted Robert, taking the opportunity to confuse his mother even more, as suggested by the look Judy gave him. Robert was all too familiar with that look. Judy had a talent of directing Robert without using words.

"What on earth do you mean?" Marie whispered in a raspy voice.

"I was here several times to visit you. Judy was with me, don't you remember?" Robert said rather sheepishly. He felt a slight pang of guilt, which was quickly overruled by the pleasure of turning and looking into Judy's sexy smiling eyes. Her eyes were hypnotic, and he loved the approving look he received when he pleased her.

Judy smiled at Robert, the "that's a good boy" smile. Of course, it was all a lie, they had not seen Marie in months. Judy loved the way she had manipulated and easily sculptured Robert into a fine trained work of art.

Marie looked confused. Just the look Judy wanted to see. She wanted Marie to doubt her own memory — so they could tell the nurse and she should run a list of tests and examine Marie and then move her to the memory care wing. But Marie was stubborn and resilient and fought back.

"Don't tell me that," commanded Marie, "I know, I remember you were not here last week, nor last month, for that matter. You have not visited me since you brought be here after Judy conveniently spilled water on my kitchen floor so that I would slip and fall." Marie spoke in a low raspy, but strong voice, she was not backing down.

Robert and Judy didn't say anything only exchanged glances—eyebrows raised as if to admit to each other that Marie was catching on to them. Before they had a chance to say anything in their defense in response to Marie's allegations, there was a knock at the door.

Judy got up from the couch, and as she walked toward the door, she glared at Marie in anger. It was Francis, the nurse, at the door. Robert and Judy were expecting her. They had arranged for Francis to show up while they were there to see Marie.

Francis nodded to both Robert and Judy then introduced herself to Marie. Francis was a psychiatric nurse, and used to patients showing resentment to participating in her mental health quizzes; because, many intuitively knew they would qualify as candidates for more drugs, and the mental ward. Francis quickly and quietly sat down across from Marie at the table where she took out her notebook and began to ask Marie questions. Silly questions, like do you remember getting up and dressed this morning? Do you remember eating breakfast?

"I'm sick alright! I'm sick from all those pills that this place pushes on me," complained Marie, becoming very frustrated. She felt she might as well have been talking to the wall, as no one paid any attention to what she had to say.

"I want to go home, Robert," Marie's face twisted as her stomach filled with shooting pains.

"Mother you can't leave here—you are home. This is the home Judy and I built for you. We have your best interests in mind," insisted Robert. Judy nodded and smirked which did not go unnoticed by Marie.

Judy watched the nurse turn the page, ready to read more questions. She read another and patiently waited for Marie to answer. Judy made Marie nervous, because she had a look on her face that said—no matter what the test revealed, it will still be determined that you are senile and need special medications and assistance which could only be provided in the memory care area of the center.

Marie must have done halfway decent on the test, or Robert and Judy just decided to ease up a little on her and let her stay in the apartment where she was living. But, they decided that Francis, the nurse, would check-in on Marie more frequently throughout the day.

So instead of moving Marie to the memory care away from her friends, they decided to have her watched more closely. They wanted her kept sedated and subdued to the point where Marie no longer had these silly notions and feeling she was trapped, being poisoned, and fed too many pills. She was too weak to fuss with them any further and merely braced for the needle she saw coming towards her.

"You sold my house and car out from under me. You stole my freedom," was the last thing Marie said before her head slumped over, and she fell into a deep sleep. Robert then ordered the nurse to check in on Marie every couple of hours.

"Keep her sedated," he suggested, "just like she is now." Robert had a commanding tone to his voice. It sounded harsh and frightened Francis, as she nodded in obedience.

Francis was a new nurse who just completed her training and had only worked at Pleasant View a very short time. She was young and inexperienced; but still, she thought Robert sounded most sinister speaking of his mother that way. It made her nervous. She made note of the pharmaceuticals Robert ordered, then quickly gathered her things and hurried out the door. Her intuition told her that something very wrong was going on. She had many questions, primarily: Why would Robert Dems, not a healthcare professional, be ordering medications instead of Dr. Charles Allen, the residence doctor?

Working at Pleasant View might have been, Francis' first job, but she soon learned that she did not like working there. She did not like the pill pushing she saw go on nor seeing the residents put into dull mindless stupors. It was very distasteful, not to mention very unprofessional. She planned on quitting as soon as she found another job. But for right now, she had other patients to tend to, there were more patients just like Marie who were sedated into a stupefied state.

Francis was suspicious, but she had not been there long enough to form an opinion of what was going on with all the pills. She was quite astute for her young age. Her second chosen career would have been one in the justice system, and if things kept going the way they were for her, she just may go back to school to add that as a second career. Her instincts told her that wrong-doings were going on at Pleasant View. She would keep her eyes and ears open.

***

Robert and Judy were doing quite well stealing other people's money. They thought they were geniuses. What a racket—it was so easy and so undetectable because people grow old and move into senior living facilities, bringing with them all their life savings. And of course, along with getting older comes aliments and ill health. It's only natural that older people get ailments—so what if it's helped along just a bit with tainted food and extra drugs. Old folks get sick, and then they die, it's all a part of life, as Robert and Judy get very rich.

CHAPTER TWENTY-FOUR

"Come on Robert, let's go!" commanded Judy heading to the driver side of the car. She decided it was her turn to drive. Robert reluctantly got into the passenger seat. He usually protested and got his way because, public appearance was very important and the man should be seen driving the car, not the woman. But today was not one of those days, because when he wasn't looking into Judy's hypnotic eyes, guilt feelings crept back into his gut.

So, today he felt bad, almost guilty for treating his mother the way he treated her. He knew Judy didn't feel guilty at all, because it was her idea to push things along a bit with his mother. But it wasn't Judy's fault that Marie was just too stubborn, too healthy, and might have stayed in her house a long time.

"I don't know about the things we are doing here," complained Robert sounding worried, "It doesn't seem right treating my mother that way."

"Robert, in case you haven't noticed, we are deep in debt," Judy glanced away from the road to look at Robert as she drove down the busy roadway.

"Well, you wanted to be rich, and you wanted it now," answered Robert not looking at her, but straight ahead to the roadway. "We could have not been so eager to get so super rich, so fast." Robert was afraid to look at Judy, because he knew that look too. No one criticized Judy. Robert knew in his gut, he would pay dearly some day for those remarks.

"We have extra money now with the sale of your mother's house, her investments, her car and other things. The opportunity was now and besides it's all over and done!" insisted Judy not liking being on the defensive.

Judy was beginning to question Robert's loyalty. In fact lately, she found a better, more devious cohort in crime, with Dr. Charles Allen. He agreed with Judy's ideas and readily agreed to increase dosages on seniors.

CHAPTER TWENTY-FIVE

Judy didn't like Robert's resistance in certain areas, like with the treatment of his mother. So she went ahead with her own plans without consulting Robert. Judy hired a more agreeable cook who would add discreet, yet very toxic secret ingredients, to the residents' meals. And she incorporated the more like-minded Dr. Allen into her plans, rather than conspiring with Robert. She no longer needed worrywart Robert and his guilty conscious.

"Well, things do seem to be working out," Robert had to admit, then became silent.

"Yes, things are working out, just look at the waiting list we have of seniors wanting to come live at our center," insisted Judy. "They bring their life savings and oh so sad if they do not seem to outlive their savings accounts. We only have to show the family a list of all their living expenses and medical care needs and it's all justified. All we have to do is leave them just enough money for burial arrangements and families have not complained."

Robert nodded; he had to agree it was a pretty slick operation. Their Swiss bank accounts were expanding—just a few more centers he thought, and they would be set for life—just as long as no one snoops around in their business.

CHAPTER TWENTY-SIX

"Hi Pete, good to hear from you," said Ann as she answered her phone and greeted her former FBI partner with a warm voice.

"By now you should have already received my reports on Robert and Judy Dems. "What do you think about what I found?" Pete asked, interested in what she had to say.

"Well, I looked it over, and I believe that I would like to visit their Pleasant View Senior Living Center that they built in Tucson," Ann replied.

"Are you sure, you want to do this?" asked Pete.

"Yes, I am sure, because I have a funny feeling Marie may be a resident at the center, perhaps held there against her will."

"Sounds reasonable," Pete had to admit. "Just be careful and stay in touch."

"I will," said Ann in an unsteady voice, which Pete picked up on.

"I'm here if you need me," offered Pete than added, "Remember Robert and Judy could be very ruthless people."

"Okay, I'll be careful," Ann said taking in a nervous breath. She appreciated the concern Pete had always expressed through the years.

"Promise?" he added for old time's sake.

"I'll keep you updated." She promised with a smile, then hung-up.

That day Ann drove the four hours from Sedona to Tucson. Heat waves rose up from the pavement in the hot desert, as she drove to the city's north edge where Pleasant View Senior Living Center was located. She had a strange feeling in the dry desert air, and although the air was hot, chills ran down her spine, as the huge ominous looking institution came into view. It had a creepy look about it that reminded her of the huge state ran insane asylums that were built years ago throughout the country.

As she drove closer to the huge iron gate entrance and guard house, her nerves calmed a bit. She felt a little more relaxed as she saw green succulent bushes, a freshly planted assortment of flowers, and the very pretty lake surrounded by grass and tall palm trees. She looked around the grounds and saw residents walking along the paths, meandering through the leafy mesquite trees, desert saguaro and sagebrush. She parked her car in the visitor's lot and walked to the main entrance.

Ann was not there to look for her friend Marie Dems, not on this trip; but rather she was there to inquire about perhaps moving in and taking up residency. The receptionist greeted her at the registration desk where she filled out a form. Then the receptionist led her to an office where a representative named Bob asked her to have a seat, and then sat behind his desk ready to interview her.

"So, you are interested in living in a senior center community," Bob stated while reaching for pamphlets from his credenza and handing them to her.

"Well, yes, I have considered it," said Ann, "and given it lots of thought."

"You will find our center features all the latest amenities for comfortable living and dining. We have full healthcare facility available. Our programs include senior investment and senior savings. We take care of your money and keep track of your spending account—for apartment, meals, and any medical care you may need," Bob had gotten right to the chase, to the meat of the project—money. He wanted to get that out of the way and make sure she understood their resident money-making policies.

"Our seniors are all very comfortable here, and we are all family," Bob continued.

"Oh, I didn't realize that I would be turning over all my retirement money to you," Ann expressed concern. But she knew that already, and Pete had set up a fake bank and savings investment account worth four hundred thousand dollars, which was enough to guarantee her an apartment at Pleasant View. Bob smiled when she told him just how much money she had available to turn over to Pleasant View Account Management Services.

"Yes, just consider us your investment directors as well as your care directors," "You will have nothing to worry about while living here. We take care of the business end, while our seniors enjoy a carefree lifestyle of lovely dining and socializing. We have an exercise and game rooms, tennis courts, and bowling alley."

"Do you have shuttles to take me shopping, if I wish?" Ann asked.

"Of course, and we welcome guests and lots of socializing.

"Oh, that sounds lovely."

"I'm sure you noticed as you drove in, that we have guards at all the entrances for your safety and security."

"It all sounds so wonderful, may I take a tour of the place?" Ann eagerly inquired.

"Why yes, I'll give you the tour myself. Now, if this is a good time for you." Bob was excited about the prospect of reeling in another resident with lots of money. Not like he was going to get a share of it, he was salaried. But he did get a bonus check one time for convincing an elderly man with a million dollars to move in and join their investment group.

Poor Mr. Henry had lots of money but no family. Bob remembered feeling sorry for him. Mr. Henry got sick and died about eleven months after he moved in. Bob smiled at the likely prospect as he got up from behind the desk walked over and held his office door open to allow Ann to walk out in front of him.

Bob led Ann down a long hall to the lounge and dining area. It all looked very modern and fancy, and she was impressed. Bob showed her the outside patio where folks were sitting at umbrella tables visiting and having lunch. As they walked about the premises, she searched for Marie among the two hundred plus residents, many of who were walking the grounds, visiting in the dining room and strolling in the hallways. She just had a feeling that Marie was there somewhere amongst them.

When Bob showed her where the apartments were, she searched the hallways for Marie. She saw people going in and out of their apartments and spotted one little woman in a pretty gray and pink print dress. The floral colors complimented her honey wheat colored hair. Ann couldn't help but notice that the woman looked like she was trying to hide a bag under her arm so Bob would not see it. Bob didn't notice her at all, he was too busy talking to Ann, and trying to find the correct key to unlock the door to the available apartment he wanted to show her.

"All apartments are fully furnished," commented Bob as he unlocked the door. Ann noticed that the woman with the bag knocked on an apartment door, and within a moment, a lovely silver haired woman answered the door, greeted the woman with a hug and led her inside. For a moment, the woman was turned towards her, and Ann got a good look at the woman who had answered the door. Was it Marie? She looked like Marie all right, but was very thin and seemed slightly dazed as far as Ann could tell. The woman was not full of life and bubbly like Marie. Ann gasped, could the woman be Marie? Ann made a mental note of the 204 apartment number on the door. She vowed to return later to visit the woman and see for sure if that was her friend, Marie.

The rest of the tour was rather interesting as Bob showed her the game room, bowling alley, theatre and so forth. Ann asked Bob again about the payment policy and he said most senior centers manage their resident's monetary matters so residents have nothing to worry about. He said the average resident savings when they come is five-hundred thousand and that on average was a sufficient amount to cover living costs while leaving families with some inheritance.

After the tour was completed Ann told Bob she was very impressed, and was ready to sign the papers, and would roll all her money over to Pleasant View and move in immediately to the studio apartment he had showed her. Bob shook her hand and smiled from ear to ear like an alley cat that had finally caught the frisky mouse.

Ann vowed to return to Marie's apartment the next day to visit Marie. She thought if she came about the same time that she saw the woman with the bag knock on her door, that she may catch Marie in her apartment. She stayed at a nearby hotel that night. The next morning Ann drove to Pleasant View and parked in the visitor's lot again. She walked into the side entrance just as one guard was leaving and another was taking his place. Neither noticed her, so she slipped right by and walked around the corner to the elevator.

Ann remembered that Marie's apartment number was 204. She quickened her steps on the second floor and walked down the hallway to number 204. She saw the same woman carrying a bag and getting ready to knock on the apartment door.

"Excuse me," said Ann in a low voice as she hurried up to the woman. "I am looking for my friend, Marie, do you happen to know her?"

"Marie?" Grace asked just about to knock on the door number 204.

"Yes, Marie Dems," Ann said then introduced herself. "My name is Ann Brock.

"Marie lives here in this apartment," said Grace, "I'm bringing her lunch."

Just then the apartment door opened, Marie smiled at Grace, and then spotted Ann standing behind her. Marie had to hang on to the door frame for she felt she was about to faint. She couldn't believe her eyes.

"Ann, is that you?" Marie said in a voice that sounded as tired as she appeared. Ann smiled with tears in her eyes and hugged Marie. She thought Marie looked very frail. Ann was afraid her good friend was about to faint and slip to the floor. After a moment, all three ladies shuffled into Marie's apartment and settled around the dining table.

"Please eat, don't mind me," begged Ann thinking Marie looked much too thin. She couldn't believe how slowly Marie moved. This was the woman Ann could not keep up with while they hiked among the red rocks, when Marie had visited her in Sedona only a year ago.

Marie was always the most energetic one of the two and chose the more difficult trails to hike. And she wanted to hike every day, sometimes twice a day, morning and evening. Ann couldn't believe her eyes as she observed this frail woman sitting across from her.

"I wondered what happened to you when I couldn't get hold of you," Ann said with concern.

"Well, I guess you discovered then that my house and everything I own was sold out from under me," sighed Marie looking as if she was about to burst into tears.

Ann listened intently as Grace and Marie spoke, she wanted to learn all she could about what was going on at Pleasant View. She knew what she suspected was true. Robert hid her away so he could use his privileges as power of attorney and sell her house and everything in it, sell her car, and take over her investments. And now at Pleasant View, it was very easy for Robert to use his healthcare power of attorney to control her care. It was very clear to Ann that Marie, a once vibrant healthy woman, was being over sedated and who knows what other drugs they were giving her to keep her quiet, confused and docile.

"I must apologize, Ann," grimaced Marie, "I'm embarrassed at my frail condition, either it's the food or all the medicines they have me on."

"Well, I knew something happened, because I knew you weren't planning to sell your house anytime soon and if you did consider moving, you said it would be to a condo," commented Ann. "I knew you weren't thinking of moving into a senior living facility."

"Well, and I wouldn't have until..." she trailed off then said, "I know my daughter-in-law spilled that water on my kitchen floor on purpose, so I would fall."

"Oh, my I had no idea," admitted Ann sounding very concerned and determined to get to the bottom of Robert and Judy's underhanded schemes.

"Yes, beware of those two, I must be careful not to say that around here or they'll have me even more sedated," said Marie, "My worse fear is being moved to the memory care wing." Marie lowered her voice because she so did not trust her environment, and assumed that every apartment was bugged.

"But I feel better now that Grace has been bringing me lunch every day," said Marie. "She knows just when to bring it, in between nurse visits."

"Yes, I have buddied up with, Ed, the guard at the south entrance, and he brings us lunch from the Deli down the street while on his break," shared Grace. "Of course we do not know how long that will last. They encourage eating every meal here. And of course, we have nowhere to go for It has become very hard to get a shuttle to go anywhere else to eat," complained Grace.

"I have resorted to not taking most of the meds that the nurse hands me," admitted Marie. "I hold them under my tongue as I drink the water, then spit them out in my hand and put them in my pocket, when the nurse isn't looking." She was trying her best to appear able to overcome her depressed environment that she was suddenly thrown into, as if cast into a lockup facility for a crime she didn't commit.

"On my," Ann said as she listened intently to both ladies, "this is a nightmare!" She was sympathetic and vowed to help.

"There is something odd about the food here," noted Grace eager to fill Ann in on all their suspicions regarding Pleasant View.

"We wonder if they add medicines right into the food. It all has a funny aftertaste," added Marie.

"At first, we thought that our taste buds were all screwed up from all the medicines we take," said Grace, and Marie nodded in agreement. "But, now we have come to suspect the food too. We were eating three meals a day but losing weight and growing ever weaker. We feel dazed and out of it most of the time. Our food from the deli that Ed gets for us tastes just fine, so it's not us; it's the food here that is weird."

Ann didn't know what to think. She couldn't believe the downward spiral and dreadful change in Marie. She could definitely tell that Marie was on heavy meds. Ann wasn't sure what her next step should be. Should she go on with her undercover plans and move into Pleasant View herself and see what happens to her. Was that even necessary when Grace and Marie told her that the food is bad, they force lots of medicines on them, and people are suspiciously dying way before their time?

Grace and Marie told her about Mr. Jones' unexpected death, and Joan's sudden death and how Margaret had deteriorated right before their eyes to the point beyond recovery. Ann made a note to contact Mr. Jones' and Margaret's family to see if they received the remainder of their love ones' money. Ann vowed to get Marie and Grace help before things got any worse.

Ann told them next time she visited she would bring some groceries. She would bring dinners with good meat, vegetables, fruit and some desserts. The ladies were filled with gratitude. Ann hated to tear herself away, but after a nice long visit, she hugged and said good-bye and promised to return soon. Her plan now was to talk with Pete and see if he found out any more information.

CHAPTER TWENTY-SEVEN

"I'm afraid I couldn't dig up anything else on Robert and Judy Dems," reported Pete. "We definitely need more evidence if you are suspecting wrong doing at Pleasant View. Right now we just have your friends' Marie and Grace's word and they could be accused of being senile and imaging that the food tastes funny, or that they suspect they are given too many medicines," warned Pete.

"Yes, I guess you are right," Ann had to admit.

"As of now we can't prove anything. What we need is an inside informant source, like a cook, a doctor, or a nurse to verify the wrongdoing and to testify in court. And, most importantly, to prove that Robert and Judy Dems are the brains behind the operation," said Pete.

"Well, I need to go back then, and speak to some of the staff, Marie and Grace are in no shape to do it. And if they try, they will be deemed senile and moved to the

"

memory care where they will be prescribed even more pills and injections."

"So, you have the proper authority, the FBI bureau will hire you back as a temporary consultant agent," said Pete, "I will get that paperwork started."

"Okay then, send me my necessary clearance to enable me to access records," Ann said with a determined smile glad to be back on the force. They talked while Pete was logging into his computer. Since Ann's info was still there it only took a few minutes to reinstate her identification from "retired" to "active," and she was in.

"Okay Ann Brock, you are ready. I got you back in," Pete promptly reinstated Ann's credentials and security licenses into the bureau's computer system.

Truth be told, she did miss the bureau and its intriguing work. Ann was energized and eager to get back into the swing of things. She knew she needed one or two good whistle-blowers that worked at Pleasant View. She had to get chummy with the employees and hopefully be hired on as a cook. It seems the worse offenses were the over-prescribing of pills and something added to the food to make people sick.

She and Pete came up with a false background as a cook with a felony record, in jail for attempting to poison her husband by adding anti-freeze to his beer. Before he had a chance to die, her evil deed was discovered when thinking he had an ulcer, he went to the doctor and tests discovered the toxic substance in his blood stream. A fictitious Ann Baker went to jail, but she got out early for good behavior. Her records showed that she learned to cook and became a chef while in prison. She and Pete figured Robert and Judy Dems would take note on her prison record, because they needed someone who was demented and underhanded enough to poison people.

"Okay, we'll go with that," Ann said as she read over her history and profile that Pete created for her."

Armed with Pete's creative resume, Ann returned to Pleasant View to apply for a job as a cook and server. She interviewed with a woman named Mary, the personnel manager.

"Good morning, Ann," said Mary, "have a seat please."

"Thank you, I appreciate your willingness to speak with me."

"I see you are interviewing for a chef's position, and that you have a very impressive resume. It's very detailed, and I like that."

"Well, I just thought that I would be up front about everything," Ann was poised and neatly dressed in a business suit, not too fancy but with the look of a big attempt to appear professional.

"You did jail time for attempted murder, for trying to poison your husband," Mary wanted to confirm her record.

"Well, that was a low point of my life, I must admit," Ann tried to sound somewhat angry but not too angry.

They sat in silence for a few seconds. Ann was a little nervous while waiting to hear Mary's response. Mary spoke in a low clear voice barely above a whisper, like the secret was just between them.

"Well, we'll just assume that the bastard deserved it." Mary was the new hiring agent for Pleasant View who was brought on board by Judy.

Ann had made an attempt to disguise herself before visiting Pleasant View because she had attended Judy and Robert's wedding as a guest of Marie's. She was afraid if Judy interviewed her, she would recognize her. So, Ann had darkened her hair and changed the style, and she wore large rimmed glasses. She felt lucky to have been interviewed by Mary, who seemed to think nothing of her deviant past.

"We have a policy here not to discriminate against anyone. We consider ours a second chance employment opportunity," said Mary, "and we are going to hire you."

Ann was in, just like that. She was intrigued with Pleasant View's hiring policies. The fact that Pleasant View hired her, a cook with a record for poisoning someone, intrigued her. Were they really that open-minded, she wondered. Open-minded, or was it indeed a clue that something underhanded was going on at Pleasant View?

Ann was pondering the thought when Mary asked a question, "Can you start work tomorrow, then? I'll have Tom, the head chef, show you around and get you started."

Ann was about to ask salary and benefit questions, but Mary beat her to it.

"You will be paid minimum wage," reported Mary, "but, we can give you a break on your studio apartment monthly fee."

"That sounds great," Ann replied, only too glad to be hired so she could keep an eye on the cooks and how they prepared the food.

"Well, Ann Baker, we will expect to see you back here in the morning then, at eight."

Ann had to get use to her new last name. She knew Pete chose the name Baker because it was pretty close to her real last name, Brock. She made a mental note to update Marie and Grace and hoped they could keep a secret. She was excited and looked forward to her new job. As soon as she got back to her hotel room, she called Pete to let him know that she got hired.

"Wow, glad to hear it," Pete was pleased that their ex-convict strategy worked. He hoped Pleasant View's personnel director would go for the convict angle. The hiring policies of Pleasant View were most generous to hire an ex-convict, or were they somewhat underhanded, and expecting Ann Baker to do some underhanded things as a cook?

Ann got up as soon as the hotel alarm went off. She wanted to arrive early at Pleasant View, in order to pick up her door pass, and employee ID tag. She met Tom, the head Chef, who was expecting her when she arrived in the kitchen. The first two hours was all about him showing her where supplies were kept, the recipes they used and the daily breakfast, lunch and dinner menus. Ann could see the menu items were pretty basic and techniques were common. If they had left over roast beef and vegetables from dinner, they would make beef vegetable soup for lunch the next day. The kitchen was run very practically. Tom skirted right past a small metal file cabinet without mentioning anything about it, so Ann asked what was kept in the cabinet. She pretended she didn't see the lock and tried to sound as casual as she could.

"Oh, I'll come back to that later," said Tom. Ann wondered if medicines that got added to foods were kept in that cabinet which stood in an out of the way, place yet handy enough to access.

"How about I'll get you started on lunch preparation," Tom suggested and led her over to where the menus were tacked to the bulletin board.

"Here's the menu for today. If you need something and can't find it, just ask. Quantities and serving sizes are also listed — so you know how much soup to make and sandwiches to prepare."

Ann eagerly went to work and found that she actually enjoyed cooking. It took her a bit to get used to cooking in large quantities, and lifting heavy pots, but she managed. She figured if pills were to be added to anything, putting them in the soup would be the easiest way to distribute them and calculate the quantity per bowl for each resident. They pretty well had it figured out about how much each resident ate at one time. A ten-ounce bowl of soup was easily emptied so she figured they would be able to calculate the dosage easily enough.

She had the soup made well before lunchtime. Tom had been watching her off and on as he did his work. He was preparing a large beef roast to put in the oven.

Another cook then called her over to show her where more pots and pans were kept.

Although he looked over his shoulder, to see if anyone was paying attention, Tom didn't notice that Ann got a glimpse of him slipping the key from the hook and unlocking the beige colored steel cabinet that stood discreetly in the corner, a few feet from the cooking area. Ann watched as he unlocked the cabinet and removed a small container. At first, Ann assumed he tasted the soup and was going to add salt. But why keep salt locked up. She watched as Tom measured a small amount of the white powder and then poured it into the soup, and then stirred well before placing the lid back on the huge pot. Tom then went on to his next task of cutting up chicken and preparing to fry it in a deep fryer.

Ann was bright and enthusiastic and made great strides toward learning her kitchen duties. Close to lunchtime, Tom announced that the soup was ready to be served. So Ann moved the pots of soup to the serving station. She had tasted the soup before Tom secretly added his special ingredient and then tasted a small spoon full again after he added it, and indeed the taste had changed; it had a slightly bitter, medicinal taste to it. She immediately put a plan into place. She filled a small container about half full with the soup got and then stuck it in her white lab coat pocket.

Everything was all set up ready for the lunch crowd, so Tom and another other cook headed for the patio to enjoy a quick smoke. The waitresses were all busy preparing the tables with place settings. Ann slipped the small container from her pocket into a paper bag she kept in her locker; it would be safe there until she got off work. Her plan then was to send the sample to an FBI lab where Pete would record the results and get back to her.

Ann loved the suspense and was excited to be back working as a contracted special assignment agent for the FBI. She had missed the intrigue and excitement and the chase of going after the bad guys. She had done very well in her thirty-two years with the bureau.

Ann enjoyed cooking and she got a good workout every day lifting heavy skillets and large pots. She found dealing with the residents very interesting regarding their likes and dislikes when it came to food. Most of the residents did not like spicy foods, and they seemed to have their favorites. Some liked the beef stew over the chicken and rice casserole. Some preferred pork to chicken. But, the soup was everyone's favorite. And, every day they had two types to choose from.

Ann kept a close eye on the locked cabinet and the key that hung on a nail behind it. She hoped one day to get a chance to swipe the key and unlock the cabinet without detection. She desperately wanted get a sample of the powder like substance that was hidden there. Every day Ann was filled with curiosity, as she watched Tom get out of the small container and sprinkle some of its contents into the soup. She was determined to get her hands on a sample of that powder so she could send a sample to the FBI lab.

She advised Marie and Grace not to eat the soup. They readily agreed, loving the idea of helping Ann get to the bottom of what was going on.

"See, I knew that there was something suspicious about the soup having a slight oddly bitter after-taste." Marie said one day right after Ann started cooking in the kitchen. Marie, always wanting to have a career in investigative reporting, was very interested in hearing about Ann's detective work.

Ann clued her in on a few things, but made Marie promise not to say a word to anyone about what she was doing. The excitement and intrigue of Ann's adventures kindled a small spark of energy in Marie. Ann was only too happy to see it. Ann was happy that Marie was feeling better and getting outdoors with her friends to walk each day. She joined them whenever she could. They walked shorter walks until Marie built up her strength which seemed to be progressing nicely.

Grace was still bringing Marie deli sandwiches she got from Ed. Both Marie and Grace continued hiding pills and taking fewer of them, so they were feeling better.

Ann was comfortable in her small studio apartment down the hall from Marie's apartment. One morning as Ann, Grace and Marie walked around the grounds. Marie expressed concern about Ann's condo in Sedona.

"Oh, I have friends to keep an eye on my condo," answered Ann, "this is only temporary anyway, until

I find out what is going on here." Ann suddenly felt bad, because as soon as she said that, she wished that she had not said it.

"I wish my stay was only temporary," Marie said sounding sad, "not that I wouldn't miss you ladies." At that moment she knew she would miss them. It was just the idea that she was forced into being there. She would have felt differently if the choice had been hers and hers alone.

"Surely your son can not hold you here against your will forever," said Ann feeling sorry for Marie and all that she had been through.

"Well, he's doing a pretty good job of it so far," complained Marie. She was mad enough to pick up the pace now, since she no longer needed her cane. She could feel herself getting stronger.

"Well, let's see what I find out from the lab about the ingredients that are added to the soup," suggested Ann. She was anxious to hear back from Pete about the findings of the lab tests.

"Yes, but if there is any tampering with the soup couldn't Robert and Judy just blame it on the chef, easily enough?" asked Grace.

"Yeah, if Robert is nowhere around the kitchen," said Marie, "how can Robert be blamed? Marie was increasingly depressed, the more she thought how cold her son Robert could be. Marie couldn't totally blame Robert. She was convinced that Robert had fallen under Judy's evil spell. No matter, Robert was her son and she was worried about him.

The ladies made sure they talked outdoors whenever they discussed the wrong doings they suspected were going at Pleasant View. They were worried that the rooms and hallways were equipped with hidden cameras and recording devices.

"I'm afraid that we must be very careful about accusing Robert, or any of the management, about any wrongdoing we suspect around here," warned Marie whispering and looking worried.

"Yes, because they would just say we were senile and put us in the memory care and give us more drugs," reasoned Grace, "We need to be very careful."

CHAPTER TWENTY-EIGHT

Ann went to work every day in the restaurant and watched as the chef "seasoned" the soup. She soon discovered it was not only the soup he was doctoring with the ingredients from the small container, but many of the other dishes, too. She wished she would hear back from Pete about the lab results of the soup sample she had provided for him. She was impatient. Pete continuously reported that the lab was evidently backed up with work.

Each day Ann waved to Marie, Grace, Betty and Alice as they came into the dining room and sat as their usual round table in the corner. Every moment she had she went to visit with them. Ann had a minute while waiting for the bread to finish baking and strolled out to say hello to the ladies. She wondered where Alice was because it was unusual for her not to be with the other ladies.

"How are you ladies doing today?" asked Ann. She was always glad to see her friends.

"We're fine," they all responded in union, but not in their usual chipper voices.

"Where is Alice today?" Ann asked as she looked at the empty chair where Alice usually sat.

"She hasn't been feeling well," Betty spoke up first.

"We think she has the flu," added Grace.

"She started feeling bad yesterday afternoon," reported Marie in a worried voice.

"We're worried about her," Betty said and was hoping they wouldn't get the flu, too.

Ann had to be discreet, but tried to suggest items on the menu to the ladies that she did not see the chef add the secret ingredient. Sometimes the ladies took her suggestions and sometimes they did not. Ann could only suggest certain items over others.

She couldn't dare suggest certain items on the menu could be poisoned to a group of gossiping seniors, for fear that they could all end up in the memory and psychic ward pumped full of more drugs. She had to have proof of any wrongdoing that might be going on in Pleasant View's kitchen. She felt she also had to be careful, for she could also end up in the psychic or memory care wards of Pleasant View; after all, even though she was an employee there at Pleasant View, she was also a resident.

After her shift, as she walked to her tiny apartment, she saw Grace leave Marie's apartment. Ann thought it looked as if Grace was crying. "What's going on Grace, is everything all right?"

"We saw the ambulance attendants wheel Alice out

on a gurney very early this morning. We just got word that she died. We saw the family come in a couple of hours ago."

"On my gosh!" Ann couldn't believe what she was hearing about Alice.

"What happened to her, why did she die?" asked Ann.

"She had the flu. Anyway, we thought she had the flu. Alice thought she had the flu too. Early yesterday morning that's what she told us when we went by her apartment to get her for our morning walk," shared Grace, "and then this."

"Oh my, how is Marie taking it?" Ann was worried about her.

"Oh, she's very distraught," said Grace, "the nurse gave her a sedative, and she is resting now."

"I guess Alice's family is taking this pretty hard."

"Yes, they are here in the building," shared Grace, "I heard them yelling in the financial department a few minutes ago before I went to check again on Marie."

"What were they yelling about?" Ann wondered. "Could you hear what they were saying?"

"Oh yes, I could hear them all right, they were very loud. They were yelling about their money — seems they thought there should be more money left over because Alice had not been here that long, I heard them plain and clear."

"Oh my, such a tragedy!" Ann said. She had an idea then, besides trying to catch Pleasant View in a food poisoning scheme, she would also have Pete look into a monetary trace.

"Workers are clearing out Alice's apartment," reported Grace, "They said a new resident will be moving in tomorrow."

"They certainly don't waste any time around here do they?" Ann replied.

"No, there is a long waiting list," remarked Grace. "People are eager to move in."

Ann was appalled when she heard Grace say people were waiting in line to move in at Pleasant View. *More like, waiting in line to be hurried to their demise,* Ann thought. She hoped that she was wrong about suspecting foul play. She didn't want to believe what she was hearing and she hoped that residents were merely dying naturally because it was their time, not their tragedy.

Ann wanted an autopsy to be performed on Alice. She hoped to speak with Alice's family, so she rushed to the office. Alice's family was still there arguing with the investment treasurer. She hoped to engage Alice's family to help solve the mysteries at Pleasant View.

CHAPTER TWENTY-NINE

Ann hid around the corner from the doorway to the financial office. She waited patiently in the hall, out of sight. She could overhear Alice's son, Joe, argue with the accountant. He demanded to know how all of Alice's four hundred thousand dollars was spent. Alice had not been living there that long and she was not sick; certainly not when she moved into Pleasant View almost two years ago. It was plain that Pleasant View did not have a decent explanation. Joe accused them of falsifying records. Ann listened to Joe demanding to speak to the top man in charge, and saying he was going to get a lawyer. He slammed the door on his way out.

"Joe," whispered Ann. "Joe," she repeated then stepped out in front of him to block his way.

"Who are you?" demanded Joe. He sounded angry, as if he had dealt with enough fools for one day, and didn't need to run into another. He was still very angry and almost pushed her aside, when he saw that she wore an employee's white lab coat with the name Pleasant View emblem embroidered on it.

"My name is Ann," she said, "I want to help you. Can we speak in private?"

Joe inquisitively looked at her for a moment, then stopped, and nodded his head. He appeared to take a deep breath and collect himself, which seemed to Ann to calm him down a bit. She knew he wanted answers as to what actually happened to his mother.

"What can you tell me?" Joe asked as she led him around the corner away from the office.

"I'm sorry about your mother," she began. "I also want to get answers regarding my suspicions. I realize this is a tender subject at a tender time. But, I need to ask you a question.

"What is it?" Joe said in a voice that reflected his disgust with the goings on at Pleasant View.

"Would you give permission for a private autopsy to be performed?" Ann asked. At first Joe looked at her strangely. He was a tall man, in his fifties Ann guessed, rather handsome in a rugged outdoors way. He looked down at her angrily, which made the hairs on the back of her neck stand on edge. She certainly did not want to make him any angrier that what he was, so she spoke quietly and carefully choose her words.

"I only want to help," Ann offered again with a slight smile she hoped appeared empathetic enough to convince him to work with her on solving the mysteries at Pleasant View.

"My mother was perfectly healthy when my wife and I moved her in here." He had tears in his eyes now and Ann saw a softer side of him emerge, which eased her apprehensions a bit and encouraged her to go on sharing her ideas with him.

"It's why I want you to authorize a private autopsy," Ann repeated in a soft voice.

"So, what is your interest in all this?" Joe wanted to know.

"A friend of mine lives here and she is suddenly very sick," explained Ann, "and another friend recently passed. We have no explanation to explain her sudden untimely demise."

"Well, I thought about having an autopsy performed," admitted Joe. "I went to the morgue where they took her body, before I came to the office to clear up financial matters. My mother was not sick, when she moved in here," explained Joe.

"Will you share the results with me when you get them back?" asked Ann.

"Sure, why not. I'll contact you as soon as I find out. You know they looked at me funny—at the morgue, I mean—when I asked that an autopsy be performed."

"Why, I wonder?" Ann was intrigued.

"Well, when I said she had lived at Pleasant View, the doctor eyes grew large, and as he filled out paperwork, I heard him mumble something about the fact that it was the third one this month to come to the morgue from there—but the only request for an autopsy," Joe said with a cautious tone. "I thought the doctor had a very

148

concerned look about him, as if he thought something was wrong at Pleasant View. It could had been my imagination, but I don't know."

Ann and Joe exchanged contact information. She told him that she lived there in apartment 210 and to either call her or come by to let her know as soon as possible when he found out the autopsy results. Joe agreed, thanked her, and they parted ways.

CHAPTER THIRTY

Ann decided to stop by Marie's apartment before heading to her own. She was walking briskly when she rounded the corner and nearly ran head on into a nurse.

"Oh, I'm so sorry, I didn't see you coming around the corner," Ann felt bad, she had knocked the clip board, papers and medical bag out of the nurse's hands. She apologized again and quickly stooped to help the nurse pick up her things.

"I should have been looking where I was going," said the nurse quietly. As Ann helped to gather her things she looked up and noticed the nurse had tears in her eyes.

"Is anything wrong," asked Ann. "Did I hurt you?" Ann could see that nurse was very young and probably not long out of nursing school.

"No, you didn't hurt me," the nurse explained. "I'm just having a tough day, that's all."

"I'm sorry, let me introduce myself. My name is Ann, and I work in the kitchen. Is there anything I can help you with?"

"Francis," she offered and held her hand out to Ann, as they both kneeled on the floor straightening papers and folders. When they finished and got up, Francis set her things down on the hall table then proceeded to get a tissue out of her pocket and blow her nose.

"Are you sick?" Ann asked. She was beginning to think everyone at Pleasant View was sick.

"Oh no, it's just my job," Francis said wiping her tears.

"What's wrong with your job," asked Ann. "You can tell me. I want to help."

"Well I can talk to you since you work here, I guess," Francis said and managed a slight smile. "I've seen you in the kitchen at lunch, you are always very nice to everyone."

"So, tell me Francis, what's going on," Ann was ready to listen.

"Well, there is something bothering me. You sure I can trust you?"

"Of course, you can trust me." Ann tried to look as sincere and kind as she possibly could, because she had a feeling Francis could share a lot of information.

"I think there is something very wrong going on here at Pleasant View," said Francis folding her tissue and stuffing it back into her pocket.

"Wait," Ann put her hand up to stop Francis from going any further. "Do you mind coming to my apartment, so we can get out of the hallway? I think it might be better, safer."

"No, I guess not," said Francis, sounding a little hesitant. She was scared but thought something should be done. Francis gathered her things and they walked down the hall a little further to Ann's apartment. Ann hurried and opened the door and led Francis in. She quickly got her tape recorder from her dresser drawer as she motioned to Francis to sit down.

"I hope you don't mind that I record your comments," asked Ann, she wanted to be sure.

"No, I guess not, but who are you really?" whispered Francis still a little doubtful, knowing she could be called as a witness, if her statement was recorded.

"Well, I would rather just say I am a cook for now, but I am doing some investigating; sort of undercover," explained Ann.

Ann went to the kitchen and brought back two glasses of water. Then turned the tape recorder on and set it on the coffee table in front of them.

"Anytime you are ready," said Ann, "just take your time."

"Well I'm new here, and in my first week, the owner, the head guy, Robert Dems had brought in his mother," Francis began to get tears in her eyes again and hesitated.

"Just take your time," encouraged Ann, her heart beginning to beat very fast in anxious anticipation as to what Francis was about to reveal.

"Anyway, the owner, Mr. Dems, told me what dosage of which pills to use to medicate his mother," revealed Francis. "The dosage was extra strong, enough to knock out a horse. I thought I heard wrong. I asked him to repeat it." Francis looked worried. "I'm new at being a nurse, and new working here. And at the time I was thinking Mr. Dems was a doctor. I later found out that he is not."

"What else did he have you do?" asked Ann.

"He had me more than double the dosage of sedatives, that Dr. Charles Allen had prescribed. Of course, I didn't question him, I felt it was not my place to question him." Francis hesitated a second taking a deep breath, then went on, "but I knew the dosage was way too much for a small woman like his mother, Marie, so I gave her half of what he wanted me to give her. It was still too strong for her size."

"Go on," urged Ann, looking to make sure her tape recorder was getting everything that Francis was reporting. This was very important news. Ann was tense with excitement of getting such good information.

"There were other medications too, that he prescribed for her," Francis added a laundry list of pills.

"And did you follow his orders?" asked Ann.

"Yes, I did," confessed Francis. "I felt it was not my place to question Dr. Allen or Mr. Dems. Guess I was worried about keeping my job."

"Would you testify in court?" asked Ann.

"Well, I guess so," Francis seemed a little squeamish, but nodded in agreement.

"Is there anything else that you can share with me?"

"All the residents here are heavily medicated,"

Francis was weeping now, "much more than what they should be, and I am not the only nurse giving out pills to the residents."

"What other nurses?"

"I only know about Cathy. I was so surprised that she and I both delivered pills to the same residents. We only discovered this in casual conversation over lunch."

"Did she or you say anything to anyone else?" asked Ann.

"No we didn't," answered Francis, "and I am sorry about that now, because I see how the residents became almost like zombies."

"Well, for the time being keep this conversation between you and me," ordered Ann. "I want a chance to get more evidence and I don't want to spook management."

Before Francis left, Ann made sure she got everything recorded that Francis had said. Then got out a second recorder and taped from the first recorder so she would have a copy to send Pete.

The information Francis offered was crucial and implicated Robert Dems. Francis promised to testify that she only followed Robert Dems orders to over medicate his mother. Ann immediately wrapped the tape in a piece of newspaper and stuck it in a heavy envelope. She quickly slipped out of the building and walked to the mailbox down the street on the corner and mailed it to Pete. She called Pete from a pay-booth near the deli where Frank went every day to get Marie and Grace lunch.

CHAPTER THIRTY-ONE

"Pete, hi, this is Ann."

"Hey, I was just about to call you."

"Did you get the lab results back on the soup sample?" asked Ann.

"Yes, I did, and you were right. The lab found that there were traces of Amanita Phalloides, or "death cap" mushrooms in the soup. A sufficient amount Amanita Phalloides mushrooms would cause gastrointestinal issues such as nausea, vomiting and dehydration and if in a heavy dose, death, within a few hours."

"I figured. If only we could get Tom Clark, the chef, to incriminate Robert Dems," said Ann. "As it is now, it would be the chef's word against Robert's. And why would the chef want to poison everyone, unless he's a psychopath?"

"Maybe Judy paid him a lot of money."

"I'll try to prove that angle," said Ann sounding hopeful.

"Sounds like you are on the right path," encouraged Pete. "Keep me updated"

"Thanks for your help, Pete, I owe you big time."

"Glad to help. Anything else I can do?"

"Yes, there is, look for a package in the mail tomorrow or the next day."

"What is it?" asked Pete sounding curious.

"It's a copy of a tape."

"A tape?"

"Yes, there is a young nurse here who told me that Robert Dems ordered more than double the amount of sedatives for his mother," Ann replied.

"Oh my," said Pete, "is he a doctor?"

"No, she thought he was at first, or worked in confidence with Dr. Charles Allen. She also discovered that another nurse, named Cathy, was also dealing out prescription pills to the same patients, so they were getting twice the double doses."

"Will Francis and Cathy testify?" asked Pete.

"Francis told me she would, we'll save Cathy as a back-up," answered Ann.

"Okay, great, I'll look for the envelope to come in the mail."

"I have the original tape and another copy hidden away. I want to make sure we have Francis' testimony. Pete, is there a way we can trace where Robert's money, or rather the resident's money, is going—like maybe a Swiss bank account?"

"That could be tough if he uses a fictitious name," admitted Pete.

"There was another resident, Alice, who had lived here almost two years that died and her son, Joe, was quite disturbed with the accounting department because he thought there should be a lot more money left over. I spoke with him after I heard him arguing with Pleasant View's accountant, telling him he's going to get a lawyer."

"I wonder if Joe would testify," Pete responded.

"I think Joe is very upset with Pleasant View, and mostly likely would testify," Ann suggested.

"Hope we can get that in writing."

"Joe also said that he requested an autopsy."

"That's good," said Pete.

"Well, we'll see what those results reveal. Hopefully, something we can use."

"I'll look for the package. Let me know what Joe's mother's autopsy results reveal, will you?"

"Yes, as soon as I hear from him, I'll call you."

"Say, how is your friend Marie doing?" asked Pete.

"Oh, thanks for asking, Marie is better. Marie's friend Grace, met a very kind guard here, named Ed, and he is getting lunch from a nearby deli for her and Marie. So they are getting better just by not eating every meal at Pleasant View. And Marie is taking fewer pills."

"Well that's good," Pete sounded concerned, "I'm glad she is better."

"Me too, it was really tough seeing her so sedated and so sick. Marie was always so active, and we enjoyed hiking so much when she came to visit me in Sedona."

"Well, I'm sure you two will be hiking together again soon when all this is over."

"I sure hope so," added Ann.

"Hey, Ann, be careful out there, watch your back," Pete was worried for her.

"Okay I will," Ann was grateful for his expressed concern for herself and Marie.

CHAPTER THIRTY-TWO

It was Sunday evening and Robert and Judy were relaxing on their patio high on the mountainside overlooking the valley below. It was a lovely evening, warm with a gentle breeze.

"So, Robert how's your mother doing?" asked Judy, sounding more annoyed then concerned for Marie's welfare.

"I don't know," answered Robert, sipping his martini, as they both sat on lounging chairs watching the sun set on the valley below. They were comfortable in their expensively decorated and landscaped three thousand square foot mountainside home.

"Well, it seems things should be moving on a lot quicker than they are. Robert heard the annoyance in her voice.

"I haven't heard from Dr. Allen lately to get his feedback," said Robert.

Unbeknownst to Robert, Judy secretly had Dr. Allen

over-prescribe medicines to Marie, and had Cathy deliver them. The prescribed medicines were even more potent than what Robert had told Francis to give Marie. Judy was impatient. She was used to getting her way in a much speedier fashion, and the waiting was making her most anxious. Judy wanted Marie out of the way because she didn't trust her.

Judy had become more sinister with each elderly death; she was secretly conniving with Dr. Allen. They had gotten away with so much; it seemed they could not fail. It was their idea to speed up the demise of several of the residents at Pleasant View in order to keep the money flow coming in. Judy was excited about the long waiting list of seniors wanting to move into Pleasant View. She saw the monetary possibilities and couldn't resist moving things along at a quicker pace.

She was paying, Tom, the chef, huge amounts of cash to add a secret toxic cocktail of his choosing to the food. She did not want to know what he used to do the dirty deeds, nor did she care.

Tom having been a cook in Viet Nam, had drawn on his Vietnamese arsenal of toxic ingredients and decided on his favorite—dried Amanita Phalloides or "death cap" mushrooms that grew in moist Asian conditions in northern California and some places in the Midwest wooded areas. Tom pretended he had to be convinced to go along with Judy's idea of deliberating poisoning people.

"I can't believe you are asking me to do this," said Tom, "now I see why you hired me, an ex-convict, convicted of attempted murder by poisoning. You only wanted me to do your dirty work."

"Well, I like to hire folks who may have a hard time getting a job somewhere else because of their past histories." Judy thought that Tom would see though that excuse, but didn't care if he did.

"I think maybe you hired me thinking that since I had been arrested for attempted murder, that I could easily be convinced to do it again—as if killing was somehow in my blood now," Tom pointed out knowing all too well that he was a rare find for Judy and she wanted to hire him for his unique skills.

"I'll make it well worth your time, Tom," Judy said as she reached in her pocket and took out a business size envelope. Tom could see that it was stuffed full of cash.

"Would, five thousand be worth your while?" Judy said waving the envelope in front of him. When Tom hesitated a bit, Judy added—"for this month." His eyes lit up when he realized Judy would pay him five thousand in cash every month, besides his regular pay. He nodded slightly then snatched the envelope out of her hands. Judy laughed. She was happy. One way or another, she always got her way.

The secret arrangement Tom had with Judy worked very well for several months until Judy was late to pay, or no longer delivered the money to him personally, and he had to go look for her. Or if she did pay, it was a smaller amount than the agreed upon amount. Judy seemed to always have some lame excuse why she was late, or why it wasn't the total five thousand dollars. Tom saw that Judy was beginning to fail on her promise. It got to the point where she only gave him a little each month to tide him over—while promising to pay him more within a few days, but never did. She was beginning to make Tom very mad.

Judy had not seen the more sinister side of Tom—but soon she would. Tom was not only mad; he was also beginning to fear he would be the scapegoat for all the wrong doings that went on at Pleasant View. He had thoughts of deserting a sinking ship before it all came tumbling down on him.

CHAPTER THIRTY-THREE

Robert was not aware that Judy went behind his back to have Tom poison people to quicken their demise. Judy was conniving with Dr. Allen. He was as ruthless as she and in total agreement when he realized the monetary advantage of a faster turnaround in residents. A sinister excitement grew between them, as they became secret partners in crime and love.

Dr. Charles Allen had partnered with Robert and Judy in the planning development of Pleasant View Senior Living Center, but he took a shining to Judy and now wanted Robert out of the way. Robert was blind to Charles and Judy's romantic collusion. Robert had his sights on making more money for Judy by concentrated efforts to build more senior centers around the country.

CHAPTER THIRTY-FOUR

Judy spent her time overseeing the operations at Pleasant View while Robert was busy in meetings with several contractors spearheading a new senior living center project. Judy spent every opportunity she had throughout the day in Dr. Allen's office.

"Hi." Dr. Allen smiled as he led Judy into his office and told his receptionist he was not to be disturbed.

"Darling, Dr. Allen." Judy wrapped her arms around his neck and kissed him.

"I love when you call me Dr. Allen." He began undoing and sliding her jacket off her shoulders. Dr. Charles Allen wasn't really a doctor. Anyone can be a doctor he discovered, when falsified papers are easy enough to get. He had a buddy in the false document business and a few other things. Not only could his buddy easily acquire false degrees and certificates, he also had ties with pharmaceutical agents who could get him expired medications, at a very low price. Pleasant View was making huge profits by overcharging residents for pills, which cost the center practically nothing.

Of all places, Judy had met Dr. Charles Allen at Max's garage. Judy kept taking her car for service and repairs to Max. She had promised him at least that much after he did such a fine job "fixing" her late husband, Roger's, brakes.

Charles was a friend of Max, and introduced himself to Judy, while he waited as his car was being repaired. Judy and Charles hit it off as they sat together chatting in the waiting room. Max could see that Judy was a big flirt. And she flirted with Charles right in front of him. Judy didn't care. She learned all about Dr. Allen and soon discovered he could be as conniving as she. It was Charles who came up with the phony doctor scheme. Robert didn't have a clue about Dr. Charles Allen not really being a doctor, nor did he know that Judy and Charles were secret lovers.

"I need you to spike up the meds for Robert's mother, Marie," She could always get Charles to agree with her plans. He was like putty in her hands, especially right after they had sex. She was that good, she thought.

"Anything for you babe, I'll make up the order and give it to the new nurse, Francis. She's fresh out of nursing school and inexperienced and won't question an order for a higher dosage.

Judy was getting a little tired of Robert's conservative ways. Let's face it; he wasn't as ruthless as she and Charles were. Judy thought about taking the money from the Swiss bank account and running off with Charles, leaving Robert holding the bag.

"I have an idea," Judy suggested, "after we get a little bit more money in our Swiss accounts, why don't we get out of the country and leave Robert holding the bag."

Charles loved the idea. But they wanted more money, and so their plan was to wait a bit until after more money came in with new residents. "Lady, you are so clever, but let's not wait too long, I'm eager to see Paris, Italy, and travel all of Europe with you."

They planned to be overseas before anyone discovered they were gone.

"We'll need passports."

"And I just happen know a guy who can make us some," Charles replied.

CHAPTER THIRTY-FIVE

Ann had just finished her shift in the restaurant and was on her way to visit Marie, when she spotted a very attractive slender young woman with red hair, in a pink suit and with matching large hat heading into an office marked "Dr. Allen." Her curiosity rose. She waited a moment and walked up to the desk outside his office and spoke to the receptionist.

"Is the doctor in?" she asked.

"Yes, but he's busy," smiled the receptionist seeing that Ann wore a white restaurant employee coat and knowing that she worked there. "He's in a meeting with Mrs. Dems, Judy, I mean," whispered the receptionist as if it were a special, secret meeting.

"Oh, okay then," whispered Ann and smiled. She had the feeling by the look on the receptionist face that Judy visited regularly.

"Shall I make an appointment for you to see the Doctor?" asked the receptionist.

"Oh, no, I'll just come back later. I just realized I have to get back to work now," Ann said, as she looked at her watch.

As she walked toward the elevator to visit Marie, she wondered what Judy and Dr. Allen were up to. No good she figured. Ann hurried because she had just enough time to stop in and visit Marie before getting back to work.

"Ann, so good to see you," Marie smiled when she opened her door and saw Ann standing there. "Come in," invited Marie and gave Ann a quick hug.

"You are looking well!" It made Ann happy to see her friend was doing so much better. Ann could see that Marie was healthier and happier. She was more alert and looked rested. Grace was there too; she had just brought their deli sandwiches that faithful Ed continued to provide for them. The ladies were busy chatting about this and that, when suddenly they were startled by a knock at the door. Marie got up from the table and opened the door to find Francis standing there holding her medical case and clipboard.

"Oh hello, Francis," said Marie, "won't you come in and join us. Grace and Ann are here too." Francis entered the apartment and Marie quickly closed the door; but not before taking a quick look up and down the hallway.

Marie was feeling pretty chipper and more like the investigating journalist she had always wanted to be. It seems that every day brought more suspense and mystery to the goings on at Pleasant View. The suspense mounted, as she and the ladies sneaked around the hallways, whispering, going outside to avoid cameras and microphones and watching and listening for clues and suspects.

"Ann, there you are, I was looking for you," said Francis, "I hoped you might be here."

"What's going on Francis? Come, sit with us," Ann said as she motioned for Francis to have a seat next to her at the table. Marie offered Francis some tea as Grace and Ann looked on ready to listen to what Francis had to share with them.

"I have a situation that concerns Marie," Francis said looking at Marie, then her eyes moved to Grace, then Ann."

"Do say, what is it?" asked Marie as she poured Francis a cup of tea. The ladies looked at Francis and then at each other, as if to ask her if she wanted to speak to Marie in private.

"I might as well tell all of you," said Francis looking concerned, stressed and just plain worn out.

"Go on then," Marie said, "wait, maybe I better sit down first." Marie was wondering what on earth could possibly bring more troubling news to them.

"Dr. Allen, prescribed an increase in the dosages of your medications, Marie."

"When?" asked Marie.

"Just about an hour ago," said Francis, "an increase that seemed way too potent for you Marie, for your weight, and your age."

"You say an hour ago?" Ann looked at each of the

ladies. "I saw Judy Dems head into Dr. Allen's office at about that time."

"What?" Marie's jaw dropped in astonishment.

"Well, it seems Judy and Dr. Allen are growing impatient, to get you out of the way, Marie. From the way the doctor's receptionist responded to me I get the idea they may be having an affair," Ann responded.

"Damn, that woman is ruthless," said Grace, looking at Marie who appeared to be speechless.

"She sure wants me out of the way," said Marie. "Why? She has all my money. I guess she wants to get rid of me so she can get another resident with lots of money to move into my apartment. There is a long waiting list. So that's the angle," Marie looked at the other ladies; her detective juices flowing. "Move them in, take their money and then kill them off!" The ladies nodded to each other in agreement.

"Looks like your suspicions are correct, Marie," said Francis and continued, "The strength of this prescription could take down a horse."

"The audacity!" Marie couldn't believe what she was hearing. "I can't believe Robert would be a part of such a horrible scheme!" She was almost in tears.

"Maybe Robert doesn't know the extent of what is going on." Ann was trying to make it a little easier on Marie, but knew she did not trust Robert either.

"I can't believe this is all happening," remarked Grace in total astonishment.

"Well, Marie, I am here to give you your updated meds that Dr. Allen ordered," shared Francis in a sarcastic tone. "You know the dosage has been increased. He did not want me to tell you that. He hinted, in so many words, that it would be for your own benefit, if you didn't know." Francis looked around at the ladies, "Pretty sinister, I must say!"

"I suspect Judy put Dr. Allen up to increasing my dosages," smirked Marie. She placed her elbows on the table, her hands under her chin, and stared in the bottom of her teacup. As if reading the tiny settling tea leaves could solve the mysteries that the apparent bleak future held. She had to process this last bit of attempted sabotage by her daughter-in-law, Judy.

"I learned from you Ann, to get proof, and so I secretly taped his verbal request to increase Marie's dosage. I made a copy of the tape and hid it. And, I copied his written prescription before I had the pharmacy at the center fill it," said Francis feeling proud of her secret detective work.

Marie raised her head; she was proud of Francis and a little envious. But, no need to be; lately they all had their shared opportunities in investigating and detective work. And they realized it was up to them to get proof and put a stop to Judy and her evil mischief. Marie only wished that her son was not involved.

"Good Job! And welcome to our little conspiracy team, Francis," said Ann. "Sounds like you are becoming a true spy, and we are all proud of you."

Without Francis to aid her, Ann was not sure how she was going to convince the FBI to go after Judy and Robert Dems, and Dr. Charles Allen. Even though she felt more confident having proof of wrong doing by Dr. Charles Allen, she still had to get more evidence on Robert and Judy.

She needed was to get someone in the finance department to prove Robert and Judy were skimming money from resident's savings. She suspected Charles and Judy and possibly Robert were in cahoots and wiring money to Swiss bank accounts. She wasn't sure how involved Robert was. Was he becoming more of a victim than a perpetrator?

Ann thanked Francis on joining the team as a potential whistle blower and witness and told her she would make a great FBI agent.

After cautioning everyone to watch themselves and not talk in the hallways or in front of cameras, Ann went on to work.

CHAPTER THIRTY-SIX

Ann flopped on the couch after work, took her shoes off and rested her aching feet on the coffee table. They immediately felt better. Working in the restaurant was hard work lifting heavy pots and dishes and being on her feet for hours. She called Pete right away.

"Hi Pete," said Ann, "glad I got a hold of you. Do you have time to talk?"

"Hi Ann, it's good to hear from you again. Yes, I can talk now," Pete said, pulling his computer closer so he could take notes.

Ann filled Pete in with what Francis told the group that morning.

"Pete, I was hoping you might have ideas for me about what you need in the way of more evidence. I think Judy and Charles are getting more desperate and I am afraid of more deaths in the community."

"I agree. I think we need samples of the powdery substance that the chef keeps in restaurant cabinet that you spoke of, because traces of Amanita Phalloides mushrooms were found in the soup. And a steady diet of that would guarantee to make the residents deathly ill, and if their immune systems were compromised in any way, would lead to sure death. But, now, I need more samples to prove poisoning is a conscious and deliberate deed and an ongoing process. You need to catch this chef in the act."

"I have a small camera I could use," contributed Ann.

"This could get dangerous for you Ann. You need to be very discreet."

"They need to be stopped," said Ann hearing herself sound angrier then she wanted to.

"Be patient," said Pete hearing the anxiety in her voice, "we'll get them soon enough."

***

Ann watched Tom as he worked in the kitchen. Being the head chef kept him very busy so it was difficult for Ann to keep an eye on him. But she watched as much as she could while performing her duties.

She was lucky; she didn't have to wait long to record evidence. She spotted Judy handing an envelope to Tom, as if he got a bonus or extra pay besides his paycheck. Ann also noticed, that he was the only chef who ever unlocked the medal cabinet and got out the small container, measured something in his hand then sprinkled the powder into the soups. She only saw him put it in the soup; but suspected he also added it to other foods, as well. She decided that she would have to watch more closely.

Ann kept her small camera in her pocket, and one day managed to snap a series of pictures of Judy handing the chef an envelope and Tom taking it. To have further evidence, Ann had to get her hands on that small container. She needed to get a sample directly from it, to give to Pete for the FBI lab to analyze.

She was scared and nervous, but it had to be done. So she put a plan into place to check the chef's schedule. She had already seen that he did not keep the key to the cabinet in his pocket but kept it on a hook behind the back of the cabinet out of sight from anyone walking past. She had to get that key, get into the cabinet and get a sample out of that little container.

CHAPTER THIRTY-SEVEN

Ann tried to call Joe, Alice's son, to see if he had the results from the autopsy. She had tried several times to call him, but only got his answering machine. She had heard that another resident had died—a Mr. Reynolds. She watched the ambulance leave to take the body to the morgue. Again she hung out near the office and saw Mr. Reynolds' daughter in tears speaking with the accountants.

The woman was clearly upset, not only of her father's death but seemingly appalled as to what the accountant said was left of her father's money. Apparently this woman had heard rumors, and Ann heard her speak of having an autopsy performed as she stormed out of the accountant's office. Ann was waiting and headed off the young woman as she rounded the corner.

"I'm sorry to bother you," said Ann, "but might I have a word with you?"

"I suppose," said the young woman wiping her eyes with a tissue.

"My name is Ann."

"Jane Reynolds." The young woman looked at Ann cautiously, noticing the white coat. "Do you work here?" she asked.

"I work in the restaurant," Ann spoke quietly as she led Jane to a more secluded corner of the hallway.

"Who are you? What do you want?" asked Jane.

"I am working here but I can't tell you who I really am yet. Were you planning on having an autopsy performed on your father?"

"Yes, I was, I just think there is something fishy going on around here."

"I'm just trying to find out myself if something is going on, but I need more data. Would you mind if I get a copy of those results," asked Ann, "here is my number and I live here on the second floor in apartment 210."

"I guess I can let you know results," the woman said, still confused about who Ann really was. "Sure, why not? I hope you tell me what you find out also."

They parted ways then each having the other's contact information. Ann walked back to her apartment and when she arrived there found Joe, standing at her apartment knocking on her door.

"Joe, how are you?"

"Fine," he smiled, "I have some news for you."

"Oh, my, come on in then," said Ann as she unlocked the door. She looked down the hallway and saw no one. Joe followed her inside her small apartment.

"Can I get you anything?" Ann asked as she motioned for Joe to take a seat.

"No, I can't stay, I have things to tend too," shared Joe. "I got the results back directly from the lab, don't know if that was proper protocol or not, but I got them, anyway. The morgue doctor who I spoke with earlier was no longer there and the new morgue doctor acted like he didn't know what I was talking about. But I had noted when I was there earlier which lab they used. I had torn off a form that had the lab phone number and address on it, so I went and got the results myself. The technician at the lab was a substitute and appeared a little reluctant to help me, but did anyway. Probably just gave me the folder to get rid of me. I must admit I was a little crabby and impatient, which was probably another reason why he just gave it to me."

"What did it say?" Ann's heart was beating fast in anticipation, wishing he would hurry and get to the point.

"I was appalled when I pulled out the form and read the autopsy results—there were traces of toxic Amanita Phalloides mushroom residue found throughout her tissues and organs." Joe looked pale.

"Oh my," Ann pretended to be astonished, "a toxic mushroom!"

"Yes, it's nicknamed the "death cap" mushroom because of its toxicity. The mushroom can be found growing wild in the woods of northern California, in Asia and some places in the Midwest. I looked it up."

"I made copies of the report for you and I kept copies for myself. I will gladly testify in court."

"I may get another report of another resident's autopsy back soon from Mr. Reynolds' daughter, Jane," Ann informed Joe.

"Who are you anyway?" asked Joe. "I mean, I don't think you're just a cook are you."

"Well, let's just say for now that I am an inquisitive resident and leave it at that. I have friends here that I am worried about," answered Ann.

"I want to go to the authorities with what I found out and because of the money. If you can assure me you are working with them I can wait. And, you certainly have reason to worry if you have friends here."

Ann assured Joe that she was in touch with certain agencies who were looking at the money and the seemingly untimely deaths.

"Let's keep in touch, then, okay? I'm getting a lawyer to help me with the money and with the autopsy results. Just let me know when you need me to testify or do anything else for you," Joe offered, as he left Ann's apartment.

Ann put a copy of Joe's mother, Joan's, autopsy results in a safe place and mailed the other copy to Pete for safekeeping. Certainly the law would be called in soon.

It was time for Ann to get back to work but she had just enough time to stop in on Marie and see how she was going.

CHAPTER THIRTY-EIGHT

"There you are," Marie said as she opened the door after hearing Ann knock her special knock, so Marie knew who it was.

"How are you today?" Ann asked as she hugged Marie.

"Just fine, Grace was just here, we had our deli lunch. What's going on, anything?" asked Marie, motioning for Ann to have a seat.

"Nothing much, just planning on going to work soon," shared Ann.

She didn't share Joe's mother's autopsy results with Marie—there was time for that later. Why get Marie all upset—besides where was no proof where Joe's mother got the poisoning, it could be another resident who visited her and poisoned her drinks or something. Ann could not prove it was food from the restaurant.

She had to get into that cabinet to find out what was in that small container. She already had pictures of Judy handing Tom an envelope. She assumed it was money. She also had pictures of Tom unlocking the cabinet and putting a small plastic container he pulled out of his pocket into it. Ann watched the whole transaction and planned on sneaking into the restaurant kitchen cabinet that night.

"Do you want to sit down for a second?" asked Marie, "You are looking a bit out of sorts today."

"Oh, just have my mind on some things I guess," Ann replied. She really didn't want to say too much in fear of alarming Marie.

"Mind if ask, what?" asked Marie.

"Well I suspect some wrong doing is going on in the restaurant, so I was planning on going back down tonight when no one was there and seeing what was in a certain metal cabinet."

"My, certainly looks like you can take the girl out of the FBI, but you can't take the FBI out of the girl," joked Marie half-heartedly, looking concerned and worried for her friend.

"I guess not." She had to chuckle at Marie's sense of humor and healthier attitude. "I'll be careful," Ann promised, as she hugged Marie and left to go work.

CHAPTER THIRTY-NINE

Jane Reynolds left Pleasant View after speaking with Ann and went directly to the funeral home. Already suspicious, she had contacted a lawyer who referred her to a private doctor who could perform the autopsy. But, when she got to the funeral home she was told her doctor never showed up. The funeral home doctor had already performed the autopsy, and found evidence of an apparent heart attack.

Jane did not know that the funeral home doctor was being paid off by Pleasant View and had grown more cautious after dealing with Joe. They altered reports after Joe threw a fit. Joe had been angry when he was at the funeral home about getting his mother's autopsy done. He wanted answers.

Dr. Brown did do an autopsy on Joe's mother and informed Joe but also informed Dr. Allen and Judy Dems. This was the first case they had where the child of a resident asked for an autopsy. They knew it was a mistake not to have considered this a possibility. They were upset Dr. Brown allowed that report to get out. Joe should not have seen the true results of the autopsy.

"Sorry boss," Dr. Brown was full of regret, "that one got away from us, I admit."

"Well, you better be more careful. We can't afford to screw this up." Dr. Allen was angry.

"Well, I don't think that the son understood what he saw."

"You better hope he didn't."

That one got away from them, but for Jane, Mr. Reynolds' daughter, Dr. Brown lied to her doctor, a Dr. Sims, whom she had paid to do the autopsy. He told him the body had already been cremated by mistake. Dr. Sims was a busy man and believed the story. There was nothing he could do even though he knew his client would be upset.

Dr. Brown contacted Jane, after making sure the body had been cremated, and told her of the dreadful mistake made by one of his newer employees. Dr. Brown knew however, that this kind of "mistake" could not be repeated more than once. He was getting a bad feeling about the future of his work with Pleasant View.

CHAPTER FORTY

Judy and Dr. Allen were having another one of their daily "meetings" in his office behind a locked door after they told receptionist they were not to be disturbed.

"Love you, Judy," Dr. Allen murmured as he lit Judy's cigarette after their afternoon sexual delight.

"Love you, too," She wondered, did she really love Charles, or only loved that they were partners in crime.

"Can't wait to get you to Paris, where we can relax all day; have sex as often as we want," He smiled as her kissed her.

"It will be so lovely, my love," she giggled and flipped her long red hair over her collar as she was getting dressed.

Just then the receptionist rang the phone.

"I told you I did not want to be disturbed," Dr. Allen told the receptionist with an angry tone.

"I'm so sorry, but Dr. Brown from the morgue is on the phone."

"Okay, I'll take it," Dr. Allen rolled his eyes at Judy as if to say, "What now?"

"Hey, Dr. Allen," said Dr. Brown, "Got some interesting news for you."

"What is it now?" asked Charles frowning as he looked over at Judy sitting on the corner of the desk. Her blouse was loosely open and slipped off her shoulder which made him want to hurry and get off the phone and back to love making.

"I'm getting tired of all these cat and mouse games about autopsies," complained. Dr. Brown. He was cursing himself for ever getting tangled up with the likes of Dr. Allen and Judy Dems.

"What do you mean, Dr. Brown?" asked Dr. Allen, "What cat and mouse game?" What Dr. Brown revealed next made him perk up, take his mind off Judy for a second, and take note of what the autopsy doctor had to say.

"There was a Jane Reynolds in here yesterday wanting an autopsy on her father," Dr. Brown said.

"And then what?" snapped Dr. Allen, getting worried.

"Well, she wanted a Dr. Sims to perform the autopsy. But we headed him off; I told him that the body was cremated by mistake. And then I had to cremate it in case he come back. But I can't make that mistake more than once, you know?"

"I can't believe all these people want autopsies all of a sudden. I will get back to you. I'm sure Jane is going to be upset when she finds out her father was accidently cremated."

"I can take care of her, but I can't do that again," said Dr. Brown. No one wanted the scheme to be discovered by the law.

Charles hung up the phone and frowned at Judy.

"What's that all about?" asked Judy looking worried.

"We need to get out of here real soon," stated Dr. Allen.

"Okay, soon, we have three new residents moving in tomorrow, totaling nearly a million bucks, as soon as we get their money and wire it to our Swiss bank account, we're out of here." Judy said, thinking of what else needed to be done. She was pleased with the plan she had put into place, but she had to admit that she was getting a little nervous. She didn't show it but she was getting concerned and anxious about being discovered. Her greed overruled her fear of getting caught, though.

"Just two more days; I have already made reservations in Paris for us. I was just waiting to make the plane arrangements till I was sure of the day."

"What about Robert?" asked Dr. Allen.

What about him?" asked Judy, "I have already moved our assets into a new Swiss account that I set up for you and me. Don't forget, we need Robert to take the rap. So, make sure all points of evidence lead to him, like the way we get our medications and how we fixed the books, and pay off the morgue doctors and the cooks. All that stuff needs to trace back to Robert. So, we can be free and clear and out of here," Judy had to laugh at the silly rhythm she made.

Dr. Allen, laughed too as he wrapped his arms around her, and with a mighty hug lifted her up off of her feet, "Free and clear and out of here," he sang.

CHAPTER FORTY-ONE

Ann woke up in the middle of the night and decided this was the night to get a sample of whatever was in the small container locked away in the mental cabinet in the restaurant kitchen. She got dressed in a flash, and quietly unlocked her apartment door. She stuck her head out, looked both ways and listened. The hall was void of any activity as far as Ann could tell. She looked both ways before stepping out into the hall. She didn't hear or see anyone, and so she quietly walked toward the stairs and quickly descended two flights down to the lobby.

Not seeing a single soul, she sneaked to the adjacent wing where the dining room and kitchen was located. She smiled as she easily slipped past the glass-partitioned guard station. No one was around, that Ann could see, just the security guard, and he was reading a newspaper.

She slipped through the dining area, then on into the

kitchen. It was dark except for a few lights on appliances which aided in her ability to see her surroundings and avoid bumping into metal pots, or knocking over food carts that would make a heck of a racket. She carefully walked over to the cabinet, reached behind it and removed the key off the hook. Her hand was shaking as she unlocked the cabinet door and quickly and quietly reached in and with the aid of her flashlight found the small container.

She got it out carefully, opened the lid and shook a small amount of powdery substance into a small empty pill bottle that she had with her. She carefully replaced both container caps, stuck the pill bottle in her pocket and returned the small container back inside the cabinet. She locked the cabinet and put the key back on the hook, and slipped out as quietly and carefully as she slipped in and returned to her apartment.

Ann managed to get a couple hours of sleep, until her alarm went off and she had to go to work. She left her apartment a few minutes early and walked to the mailbox to mail Pete the envelope that contained the small pill bottle.

CHAPTER FORTY-TWO

At Judy and Robert's mountain side home, the phone rang with an annoying trill. It was the third time in two hours it had rung and the third time that Robert had let the call go to the answering machine. He sat at his desk in his home office in deep thought going over a list of his assets. Something was not right with the records. He was going to have to speak to Judy about it.

The speaker on the answering machine announced the caller. To Robert's annoyance, it was his mother. She left the most irritating message, Robert thought, demanding he get the doctors and nurses to stop pushing pills on her. Robert could tell, much to his dismay that his mother certainly was not taking all of her medicine that he had Dr. Allen prescribe for her. Oh, he knew well enough because if she did take all those medicines, as he wanted her too, she wouldn't be calling and sounding so annoyed.

It was exactly why he had prescribed the heavier

doses of medicines, because he knew if she was not heavily sedated, and realized what was going on, she would be very upset. Of course, it was Judy's idea! She knew Robert was power of attorney, and realized that if his mother had an accident, and he sold her house, her car and everything she owned, that Marie would clearly be annoyed, so heavy meds were a necessity.

Robert could barely concentrate on the figures he was looking over to decide if he had enough to hire contractors to build another senior living center. He decided to call Dr. Allen.

"Hello, Dr. Allen speaking," Charles, said after the receptionist put Robert through. Judy had just gotten dressed and left his office, so he was accepting calls once again.

"Charles, Robert here."

"What can I do for you?" asked Charles, straightening his necktie, and slipping on his lab coat. Charles had to smile, for at that moment he felt like the fox that got into the hen house, having just had sex with Robert's wife. He knew Robert didn't have a clue.

I need you to make sure that Marie, I mean my mother, is actually taking her medications."

"I just had Francis up her dosage," explained Charles, "Surely that should have been enough." Charles was puzzled and wondered if Robert trying to actually put his mother into a coma.

"Are you sure she is giving Marie stronger pills?"

"Well, I prescribed them, but I can check with the nurse," suggested Charles.

"Maybe you better talk to her," agreed Robert.

"Will do," said Charles and hung up the phone. Charles thought he had a better idea. Rather than speaking to Marie about taking her medicine, he might talk to Tom, the head chef about fixing Marie a special meal. He called down to the kitchen and a woman answered.

"Hi, this is Dr. Allen; can I speak to Tom?" he asked.

"Tom isn't here right now," answered Ann. "Can I take a message?"

"Yes, I need a blue-plate special sent to Marie Dems — apartment 204.

"A blue plate special?" repeated Ann trying to keep her tone normal, as if she knew what he was talking about. She had never heard of a blue plate special.

"Tell Tom," said Charles, "He'll know." Charles was beginning to get annoyed. He was in a hurry to get out of the office and meet up with Judy. They were getting together at his place to make plans for their Parisian escape.

"Yes sir, I will do that."

"He is there, right?" asked Charles.

"He is here," said Ann, "He just went on a break."

"Okay, good," said Charles and added, "send that up to her right away."

A minute after Ann hung up the phone Tom was back and saw Ann's written note ordering the blue plate special for Marie Dems.

"I'll get on this right away," Tom said, as if he was quite familiar with the order. An order that oddly enough was not listed on the menu. Tom quickly took the order slip and went about preparing the meal.

"I'm not familiar with that dish," Ann said to Tom. She was about to ask what a blue-plate special was when Tom jumped in to explain.

"Oh, it's just a special order of bacon wrapped filet mignon, with loaded baked potato, and a vegetable and we prepare it special and deliver it — that's all."

Before Tom proceeded, he gave Ann special chores to do out in the dining area to get her out of the way. But, Ann figured he was up to something and when she heard it was for Marie she tried to stick around to watch Tom. She watched him wrap foil around a potato and steam some broccoli; he already had the bacon wrapped filet mignon on the grill. Ann rounded the corner out of Tom's sight but turned back to watch as Tom reached for the medal cabinet key and opened it and took out the small container heavily sprinkled his special seasoning to everything on the plate. The plate was ready and Tom signaled for a waitress to deliver it to Marie's apartment. He then turned his attention to Ann.

"Ann, come here," he ordered. Tom was leery of Ann, she watched too closely, so he wanted to distract her and keep her busy while the waitress delivered the tray with the plate of food, drink, and dessert to Marie.

"What's up?" asked Ann.

"Come here. I want to show you how this new juicer works." Tom appeared thrilled with the new top-of-the line juicer he just bought for the restaurant.

Ann walked over to where Tom was standing waiting to show her what he was doing. As she walked his way, she wondered if he really wanted to show her how the juicer worked or if he had an alternative motive, which was to distract her and keep her busy so she couldn't chase after the waitress who was delivering the special meal to Marie.

Ann was worried for Marie, but had no way of warning her to be leery of the food being delivered to her. Her worry for Marie had her all confused and she couldn't think straight. She was trying to listen Tom explain the new industrial size juicer and trying to remember—did she really see Tom open the cabinet and put some of the stuff from the small container in Marie's food order?

This was all becoming too much for Ann. Her worry for Marie was clouding her thinking. If only Pete had gotten back to her sooner with those lab results. She wanted to punch Tom in the face and shut him up and run after the waitress to stop her. But her feet were planted, because she couldn't allow herself to blow her cover.

CHAPTER FORTY-THREE

"Coming," Marie called out in a low voice as she got up from the couch to answer the door. She wondered who had come to see her and was surprised when she opened the door to find t was the waitress from the restaurant.

"Hi Marie," greeted the waitress, "I have a special order for you, compliments of your son and Dr. Allen," The waitress was pleasant and smiled as she set the tray with covered dishes on the kitchen table. Even covered, the appealing aroma escaped from the dishes and filled the room.

"Sure smells good," smiled Marie. "I was just about to get ready to go downstairs to the restaurant. I guess you caught me just in time."

"There's a note here, too," added the waitress, whose name Ginger was displayed on her uniform nametag.

"Oh my, from Robert," smiled Marie as she picked the note up and slipped her reading glasses on, while

Ginger set all the dishes on Marie's table. It was a sweet note from Robert, apologizing for being too busy to call her back and hoping that this special delivery meal helped make up for it. Of course, Dr. Allen had told Tom to write the note and what to put in it.

Marie was all excited and thanked the waitress who took up Marie's offer to sit with her for a few minutes while she ate. Having been on her feet all day, the waitress gladly accepted the invitation. They chatted about this, that, and the weather. The young waitress was a bit of a chatterbox and told Marie all about her new beau and the lovely jewelry he gave her. Marie was well entertained while she ate her delicious dinner sent special order from Robert. When Marie finished, Ginger removed the dishes and left Marie's apartment.

While struggling to carry everything Ginger did not pull the door all the way shut, thinking Marie would shut it. But Marie was feeling a little light headed. Shouldn't have gotten up from the chair so fast, she thought. A nap, she felt she needed a nap.

Leaving the door ajar turned out to be a blessing. Ann was very concerned about Marie. She planned to head to Marie's apartment as soon as she could get away from Tom's tutorial on the one hundred and seventy functions of the giant juicer. He talked for what seemed like an hour, as Ann stood and tried to concentrate with frayed nerves. She wished Tom would hurry up so she could get out of there on check on Marie. She was so worried about Marie she wouldn't be able to remember half the stuff he told her anyway.

Finally, Tom finished his lecture and she could break away from his pontificating grasp. She walked to the hall, so Tom wouldn't suspect anything. But, when she cleared the corner and was out of his sight, she raced over to the stairs not bothering to wait for an elevator. In a few seconds, she was there on knocked on door 204, Marie's door. The door was not latched altogether and swung open when she knocked on it.

"Marie?" Ann called out again and again as she looked around the apartment. She looked and listened for signs of Marie. She looked into the bathroom, she wasn't there. Instead, she found Marie in her bedroom lying on the bed. Marie appeared to be unconscious. Ann quickly approached her and tried to wake her up shaking her shoulder. She called her name over and over again and shook her. Finally Marie moaned a bit. Ann ran to Marie's phone and called for an ambulance. She gave the dispatcher Pleasant View's address and Marie's apartment number. They were on their way. She then called down to the guard's desk and told the guard to be expecting an ambulance soon for room 204.

Much to Ann's relief, the ambulance arrived in minutes. The attendants rushed in and immediately examined Marie. They found low vital signs, a weak pulse; her body was in stress. They quickly carted her to the elevator and out to the ambulance. Ann stayed by Marie's side and rode with her in the ambulance to the hospital.

CHAPTER FORTY-FOUR

The ambulance attendants quickly rolled the gurney from the ambulance into the emergency room where doctors had already gathered and were quickly briefed on the status of her condition. The doctors seemed puzzled when Ann informed them that Marie recently ate and wondered if there was something wrong with the food. With further examination, the doctors concurred it appeared it might be food poisoning symptoms, and prepared to pump her stomach. They would to send samples to the lab.

They reported back in a few minutes that they found traces of strong sedatives. They also found a substance that really threw them off for a minute because they were not familiar with it. Seems Marie had eaten poison Amanita Phalloides mushrooms, and they luckily caught it in time before Marie fully digested the toxins, and that this saved her life.

Ann of course, stayed in the hospital, at Marie's side, until she started to regain consciousness.

"Oh, I owe you so much, Ann," Marie said weakly, when she finally regained consciousness, "I believe you saved my life." Marie spoke in a harsh whisper because her throat hurt from the tube they had fed down her throat and esophagus in order to pump out her stomach contents.

"I'm just glad you're okay," smiled Ann, "I am so glad I got to you when I did."

"You know what," smiled Marie, "I think I am ready to move to Sedona like you wanted me to."

"Finally," laughed Ann, leaning over the bed to kiss Marie's head.

"But, first let's put these bastards in jail!" Marie said in a determined voice. She should have felt weak, but she was suddenly full of determination and spite.

Both Marie and Ann knew that they had evidence now to put Tom, the chef, away, and possibly Robert, Judy and Dr. Charles Allen. Marie hated to see her son involved in all the wrong-doings. It appeared that there was no way Robert was going to escape being part of the Pleasant View's pill pushing, toxic food scheme.

Ann stayed in the hospital room with Marie. And helped Marie sit up to sip on some lemon-lime soda and ate a small amount of Jell-O, which seemed to help settle her stomach and give her some strength.

Ed, the south entrance guard, came to the hospital to check on Marie. Not only to see how his good friend was doing; but, also, to give her some bad news. He tried to break it to them gently, but he was in tears. Because much to their sorrow and regret, they learned Grace had also received the blue plate special, had taken ill and was rushed to the same hospital, where she died without ever regaining consciousness.

Traces of the toxic mushrooms were found in her stomach, too. Apparently Grace received more of the mushrooms and her immune system was just too weak to overcome the fast acting toxicity.

Ann and Marie were beside themselves with sorrow and anger when Ed broke the news to them. Ed was furious and told Ann that he was ready to testify in court that he got lunch for Grace and Marie every day because they thought the food had an odd taste to it and was afraid to eat it. Ed wanted to go after Robert and Judy Dems and Dr. Charles Allen.

CHAPTER FORTY-FIVE

"Charles, what's up?" Robert asked, he knew he sounded cross when he answered his home office phone, but he didn't care.

"Just wanted to let you know," said Dr. Charles Allen, "that your mother is in the hospital."

"She's dying?" asked Robert surprised at the sound of his voice being more business-like than more emotionally concerned. *What kind of a son am I?* he wondered. He knew he sounded like he wanted to get her out of the way. Just what kind of a monster was he turning into?

"No, she is not dying, quite the contrary, she is recovering. But, you need to get right down there," Charles was talking fast and matter-of-factly to Robert. He spoke in a hurried voice, although he was not trying to sound hurried, he was. He was quickly packing papers in his brief case that he could not leave there in the office that might arouse suspicion. If they were found, they would implicate him in every wrong-doing at Pleasant View.

His clothes were packed and he was getting ready to meet Judy and catch a flight from Tucson to New York and then another flight to Paris. She was already at the airport waiting for Charles.

Judy had opened another Swiss bank account, in a fictitious name, and had transferred all the money, millions of it, in her new account. Robert was left with nothing but bills and a trail of evidence implicating him in falsifying resident's accounts. Charles had doctored papers leading suspicious actively to Robert. Robert would get all the blame for buying outdated pills from the black market.

"Okay, I'm on my way to the hospital," Robert told Dr. Charles as he hung up the phone and ran to his car. When it came right down to it, Robert was worried about his mother. As he got into the car he wondered why he let Judy talk him into so many underhanded schemes like pushing extra pills and drugs onto his mother and the other residents. He wondered where Judy was, he had not heard from her, and she was supposed to be home several hours ago. The wheels spun in the loose gravel as he turned out onto the mountain road leading down into the valley.

Robert drove like a crazy man, sliding around corners. He had a heavy foot, and a series of speeding tickets to prove it. Seems the longer he was married to Judy, the crazier he drove. It gave him a sense of somehow being in control of his life. But on this particular day, he was more reckless than usual as he took the curvy mountainous roads daringly fast, as if to test fate. It didn't take long before Robert realized that he had been pushing his luck.

At the first sharp curve, he noticed the brakes felt soft and he had to push harder on the pedal to slow the car. He smelled oil. Brake fluid was leaking from the brake lines. He was going much too fast to take the mountain curves safely and he knew it. He pulled on the hand brake, but it had no effect. Instead, his sports car picked up speed as he tried to maneuver the curves. His knuckles turned deathly white as he gripped the steering wheel as tightly as he could to keep the car from swinging, swaying down the mountainside. The tires skidded and squealed on the paved road.

By the third sharp curve, he had no brakes at all, no matter how hard he pumped, or stomped on the brake pedal. He screamed as his car crashed through the guardrail and took flight. His screams echoed throughout the canyon as the car veered out of control and tumbled end over end down the mountainside. Robert's screams subsided as he passed out, and he didn't see imminent death face him. Robert died in a fiery pile of rubble at the bottom on the canyon.

Once again, Judy's mechanic, Max, did a great job. He had sabotaged Robert's brake lines, just as he did for Judy's first husband, Roger. And Max, the mechanic, would do it again for Judy if she ever wanted him to.

Max was a simple minded, beer-drinking guy, who had never seen the likes of Judy before. The first time she came into the shop to have work done on her car, he was so stricken by her beauty, he knew he acted like a schoolboy. He was a married man with five kids and a ton of bills and she paid him very handsomely. It was the money as much as it was the way she looked. She dressed in flashily clothes and flirted with him. Her kisses sent him wild. He would have done anything for her. He was getting her husband out of the way so she could be with him — or so he thought.

Judy knew Max was in love with her and she strung him along so he would do favors for her. Max was the mechanic that restored Robert's old 1953 Corvette sports car. Robert had seen it at an estate sale he attended with Judy. It was sitting up on cinder blocks, had some body damage and the engine needed overhauling. Judy talked him out of it that day, but later she bought it and found Max a mechanic who restored Corvettes.

Judy had given Robert the old Corvette for his birthday when he turned fifty. He was so surprised and thrilled. Little did he realize it would be the means of his demise!

CHAPTER FORTY-SIX

Unpacked and all settled in their hotel in Paris, Judy and Charles walked arm in arm sightseeing along the Louvre Museum. They toured the DaVinci's Mona Lisa exhibit and other fine historical works of art. They were smiling and in love, taking in the sights drinking fine wine and lunching on buttery croissant delicacies served in quaint cafes.

"It's so exciting to be free and independently wealthy," Judy exclaimed.

"And in love," added Charles. He had waited for Judy to say it, but she didn't, so he did. After a while, when they grew tired of walking and looking at all the sights, they stopped at a market and picked up salad, and pasta fixings, French bread and wine and returned to the villa they had rented. They cooked, then sat on the terrace and enjoyed a romantic dinner and a fine bottle of wine as they gazed at the stars and the dazzling romantic city lights.

"I love Paris, don't you?" Judy asked as she kissed Charles and they clinked glasses and celebrated their love for each other and their love for Paris.

"I adore Paris—and you," said Charles then added, "it's time to celebrate." He reached for the bottle of Dom Perignon, popped the cork and filled their glasses, then raised them for a toast.

"To new beginnings," proposed Charles.

"To new beginnings," Judy repeated as they clinked glasses, kissed and sipped.

They were high on champagne, rich, and free to travel the world. Although it would be difficult to pull away from the City of Lights, their plan was to move to another villa on the French Rivera where they would stay for a while to see the sights and then travel on from there. They intended to travel wherever their hearts led them. The plan was to keep moving. They convinced themselves that the FBI and CIA would give up on them after they lost their trail.

CHAPTER FORTY-SEVEN

After the hospital pumped Marie's stomach and found traces of toxic chemicals and poison mushrooms, they called in the police. Upon learning that Marie came from the Pleasant View Senior Living Center, the law took over Pleasant View, and Tom, the chef, was arrested. Ann had received Pete's toxicity report which confirmed the toxic substance came from the small container in the medal cabinet.

It was quite a day for the residents at Pleasant View when the police and social workers came in and took over the facilities. The residents were concerned about what happened to the money they gave Robert Dems, and what would happen to them. According to the evening news, police received more reports from residents who were suspicious and thought the food always had a metallic taste. They complained too about large amount of medicines pushed on them on a daily basis.

Robert's fiery crash made television news and headlined the newspapers, and investigations into his death were under way. The search was on for his wife Judy who police suspected was on the move with Dr. Charles Allen. Both were missing. Marie was saddened by the whole ordeal.

"What a nightmare this whole experience has been," complained Marie to her best friend Ann who sat by her side.

"I know, it's been a nightmare," Ann said as she held Marie's hand while they watched the news on the hospital television.

"Poor Robert," said Marie after hearing the horrid news of his deadly car crash, "I think he always tried to measure up to his father's expectations, which was impossible. Just as he tried to measure up to Judy's expectations which was impossible." Marie was speaking through her tears feeling so sorry about her son's wasted life.

"That Judy is such a bitch," Marie unknowingly echoed Robert's last words that he yelled through screams right before he passed out and crashed into a fiery heap of metal.

"Such a sad thing," Ann expressed her grief knowing it was an especially tough day for Marie; first the doctors had to report to her that she had been deliberately poisoned, and then they had to give her the sad news about Grace dying and her son dying in a car crash.

"Guess the jig is up," said Marie, "for some of them anyway."

"Yes, Tom, the chef, should be in custody," reported Ann, as she sat by Marie's hospital bed and poured her some ice water from the pitcher on the stand near the bed.

"And the police, FBI and CIA are searching for Dr. Charles Allen and Judy Dems," added Ann watching Marie take a healthy sip of the ice water that soothed her aching throat.

Marie and Ann talked about the future. The plan was to move Marie to Ann's condo in Sedona. She only had a few things. Ann was happy to have Marie move in with her. Ann already had a room set up for Marie when she visited and used to hike. So, all Marie had to do was just move right in.

CHAPTER FORTY-EIGHT

"Pete, what's up?" asked Ann when Pete called the hospital room. She was eager to hear what he had to report regarding the investigation of Judy Dems and Dr. Charles Allen. "Do you have any news for me?"

"Oh, I have lots of news; but, we think that we can't touch them," confessed Pete.

"What do you mean," asked Ann sounding disappointed, "we can't touch them?"

"We believe that they left the country under assumed names and fake passports."

"What makes you think they left the country?" Ann asked.

"We checked the tapes on security cameras throughout the airport, and matched security tapes at the gate for the flight leaving for Paris," said Pete sounding exhausted. "It took some time; but, we ended up concluding that Dr. Charles Allen and Judy Dems took a flight to New York, where we found them again on security tapes at

La Guardia Airport and flight tickets to Paris matching their obvious alias names of Mr. and Mrs. Charles and Judy Albright. We also discovered that Charles has been posing as a doctor and that his certificate and license are fakes. Evidently they had someone forge Charles's physician license, certifications, degrees, and his and Judy's passports and new identifications."

"What's the next step?" asked Ann.

"Well, I'm not real sure; but, if I can work it out, I plan on going to Paris and bringing them back."

"Can you even do that?" Ann wanted to go with him, but knew she had to get Marie settled in Sedona.

"I can certainly try, besides it's been a while since I have toured Paris and surrounding areas."

"Have you found any evidence of foul play in regard to Robert Dems' death?" asked Ann.

"As a matter of fact, I was just about to tell you. The FBI and local police ran forensic tests."

"Did they find anything?" Ann was eager to learn the truth of how Robert died.

"Yes, seems the brake line was cut," explained Pete. "The distance between his home and those steep curves was just enough of a distance for the brake fluid to drain and he had no brakes at all just when he needed them the most around the winding mountainous curves."

"How horrible," said Ann then listened as Pete continued.

"The inspectors were glad to find that when the car crashed it broke into little pieces and parts of the braking system were found several yards away. Inspectors were happy to find a good length of brake line intact except for the area that was cut. The cut appeared to have been sharp, clean, and deliberate. So it had to be cut by a mechanic who knew what he was doing, so the fluid would drain slowly. We have a team questioning local mechanic shops to see if we can get anyone to talk."

"This is a mess," said Ann wishing it was all a bad dream and would go away.

"It sure is," Pete, agreed, "it appears they were all in cahoots. We have suspicious actions committed by Robert Dems, Judy Dems, Charles Allen and Tom Clark. They were all in on the wrong-doings that were going on at Pleasant View, like stealing money from residents, adding toxic ingredients to foods, and over prescribing medications. Charles and Judy will spend a very long time in prison."

"What if they are long gone?" Ann was worried Charles and Judy would get away for good.

"We'll do our best to find them, and get them back here in the United States," Pete said with determination

CHAPTER FORTY-NINE

Robert's body was completely incinerated in the crash. Marie had no funeral or memorial for Robert. He was just gone. Ann thought that was what bothered Marie the most. When Marie was up to it, Ann and Marie went back to Pleasant View to gather Marie's things from apartment 204 and Ann's things from apartment 210. As they walked the halls, an eerie feeling gripped both of them. To think all this evil went on right under their noses. People had high hopes of a life of carefree living at Pleasant View and what they ended up with was misery, monetary loss, and failing health brought on by continuous over medicating and poisoning of the food. Unsuspecting people were taken advantage of and lost everything, even their lives.

It didn't take long to box up the few clothes and other items that Ann and Marie had at Pleasant View. Then they drove four hours to Sedona.

"You sure you have enough room for all my stuff,"

Marie asked as she turned and looked at all the stuff piled up on the back seat, which was the overflow of things that they could not get into the trunk of the car.

"You don't have that much stuff," smiled Ann glad to have her companion with her. Marie smiled, too. Then they both laughed, because the car was totally filled.

"Seems, I should have moved up here the first time you asked me to, after Frank died. I'm sorry now that I didn't."

"Well, who would have thought that all those horrible things would have happened."

They had lots to talk about on the drive to Sedona. But all the bad things were forgotten as soon as they crested the last hill on Highway 89A from Cottonwood heading east into Sedona.

"Oh my, those red rocks," smiled Marie, "I had forgotten how beautiful and majestic they are."

"Yes, they have such a majestic presence," smiled Ann, "The energy, the beauty is so astonishing."

"Come on," smiled Ann as soon as they pulled up to Ann's condo, "let's just carry in what we can and unpack the rest later." She was so glad to be home.

"Sure, if you need to rest," Marie said with a grin. She was feeling pretty chipper as she filled her arms up with a big stack of clothes. "Who needs rest? What do you say, we go for a hike in Boynton Canyon?" suggested Marie, "I suddenly feel very energized, must be the vortex of these beautiful red rocks," All the medications that were forced onto Marie had finally left her system and she was so happy to be her old active self again.

"Sounds like a plan," said Ann. They dug out the hiking clothes, sticks, backpacks, and boots and were ready to go in minutes. They stopped at the market and bought some groceries and packed a lunch.

Ann drove several miles to Boynton Canyon. She was a little concerned about Marie because it had been a while since Marie had been active. So, they choose one of the less challenging trails to hike.

"Dead Man's Pass—you sure you want to hike Dead Man's Pass?"

"Wouldn't that be awful, to have survived a knock on the head, the effects of powerful drugs, and poisoning, only to be found dead on Dead Man's Pass?" laughed Marie. Ann hugged Marie and they both laughed as they headed out on the trail.

Ann knew the trail was mostly flat and not too challenging. They hiked until they found a large flat stone that was perfect for sitting and sharing, vegetables, fruit, cheese and crackers. They sat in the warmth of the sun and thanked the universe for being alive. They looked around and marveled at the silence and stillness of the canyon, the blue sky, and the beautiful desert surrounding them, filled with huge red rock formations, twisted mesquite trees, and various cacti bloomed with yellow, orange and pink flowers. It was quiet and peaceful as they sat and ate their lunch and counted their blessings.

***

"It is so good to be here," smiled Marie letting the sun warm her and the beauty of the area mesmerize her. A moment of silence between them passed, then out of the blue, Marie spoke up and Ann knew that peaceful hiking days were going to be put on hold for a while.

"You said Pete was going to Paris," stated Marie.

"Yes, I did."

"I want to go to Paris, too and get them," demanded Marie.

"What?" Ann was surprised and couldn't believe what Marie was proposing.

"I want to go to Paris," insisted Marie, "and get those two."

"You can't be serious," asked Ann.

"Those two ruined my son's life—stole it from him," Marie said in a low angry voice. She spoke as if she was her old self. All the drugs had worn off; but what Marie was suggesting sounded as if she was totally out of her head to Ann.

"Just what would we do if we went to Paris and found them?" Ann wanted to know.

"Well, we can lead Pete to them," suggested Marie.

"Judy and Charles do not know Pete, so he can easily track them without detection," offered Ann, "but, Judy knows you—and Judy knows me, remember I was at their wedding? It's why I had to darken my hair and wear the wide rim glasses as I sneaked around Pleasant View, so Judy wouldn't recognize me. We couldn't get very close to them at all; and what if they see us first and take off—we'll never get a hold of them."

"Well you have a point," said Marie, "still…"

CHAPTER FIFTY

Ann was mistaken when she told Marie that Tom, the cook, was in custody. On the contrary, Tom was long gone. He had escaped along with three other prisoners who had just completed digging a tunnel through a cellar underneath the building. Being a free man once again, Tom had plans to get the money Judy owed him. Before they left Pleasant View, he had overheard Judy talking to Charles about making plans to escape to Paris. So, he knew right where to go.

Tom contacted an old army buddy, Jack Monroe, who ran a small restaurant in Paris not far from the Louvre. The timing was perfect; Jack had just lost a cook and certainly could use another chef. Tom needed to get out of the country, and Judy and Charles were in Paris, so working for Jack was perfect. Tom figured he deserved so much more money from Judy for doing her evil dirty work. He planned to search for her and Charles in Paris.

"Welcome, to Paris and welcome to my humble restaurant," greeted Jack as he struggled to pass waitresses and guests to give hug Tom a quick hug. The restaurant was busy, and Jack motioned for help to take over in the kitchen while he showed Tom around the restaurant and the kitchen, before he led him upstairs to show him the recently vacated apartment which would be his.

"This is great, man," Tom thanked Jack as he threw his travel bag on the bed and began to unpack the few clothes he had. The place was small, but it had everything he needed. "Well, that only took a minute., I'm ready to get to work."

"Great, because I sure can use the help this evening," said Jack as he led Tom down the stairs and headed for the kitchen where he handed Tom an apron.

"Let's get to it, then," said Tom.

Jack quickly showed Tom the layout of the kitchen then they got to work serving customers as fast as they could. Jack's restaurant was catching on fast after the local newspaper did a piece on his restaurant claiming it one of the best in the popular tourist area near the Eiffel Tower and the Louvre.

CHAPTER FIFTY-ONE

"I could live like this forever," smiled Charles lying in bed with Judy, the terrace doors open, and wonderful gentle breeze filtered into their bedroom. With the gentle breeze drifted in the sweet aroma of fresh baked pastries and croissants from the shop down the street from their apartment.

"Me too," agreed Judy as she kissed him and snuggled in his arms.

"We are as free as those birds," pointing at a couple of doves sitting on the rail outside their terrace.

"Man, something sure smells good."

"Must be the bakery right down the street."

"What do you say I run down there and get us some croissants?" suggested Judy. Paris seemed to agree with her, she was feeling very energized.

"Sure," said Charles, "sounds wonderful."

It didn't take Judy long to slip into a loose-fitting blouse and a pair of Capri pants and sandals. Charles had to smile as he lay in bed watching her, seems it took her a longer time to put on all her bangles, and beads, and large loop earrings than it took her to get dressed. She piled her curly red hair high on her head and grabbed her sunglasses and purse.

"I'll be back in a minute," she smiled and kissed him before heading out the door.

Judy took the steps down to the street, walked a few doors down and was about to enter the pastry shop, but not before glancing into the shop window to see how busy it was and if there was a long line. Her heart jumped in her chest when she spotted two women who looked awfully familiar. She quickly composed herself and moved out of sight to wait for the two women to leave the shop.

"It couldn't be, could it?" Judy said to herself as she waited impatiently. She lit a cigarette as she watched the pastry shop. People were coming and going. Finally, the two women left the little shop with their bags of goodies, smiling and walking arm in arm they crossed the street.

"Oh crap," sighed Judy. It was Marie and her friend Ann. She was sure of it. Marie was alive? She actually looked quite well. How could that be? Charles had Tom cook the blue-plate special dinner for her. And what in the world were they doing in Paris? She and Charles would have to talk this over.

She waited until they walked away from the shop and were far enough ahead of her then began to follow them. She got her scarf out of her pocket and quickly covered her hair, hoping that the scarf and big sunglasses would be enough of a disguise.

She watched Judy and Marie stop in the park across the way. They sat on a bench and ate the pastries they bought. Judy watched nervously from another park bench behind some bushes. After a few minutes they got up and leisurely walked into a nearby hotel. Judy followed and watched through the hotel window as they stopped at the desk. She slipped in the door and stood behind a pillar as the desk clerk spoke to them. When they moved away from the desk, as if heading to their room, Judy followed them up the stairs, staying at a safe distance. She saw them enter a room down at the end of a hall on the third floor. Room 306.

She quickly turned and headed back down the stairs and slipped out a side door and down the street to the pastry shop. She bought the croissants, and walked the short distance to where she and Charles were staying.

"What the heck, took you so long? I was getting worried."

"Here's the croissants," Judy said as she sat on the bed and handed the bag to Charles.

"They smell good," Charles said as he reached in and grabbed one.

Charles noticed that Judy looked worried about something. "What's going on? You look like you have seen a ghost."

"I have seen a ghost."

"What?" Charles was befuddled.

"Marie is here in Paris!"

"What?" Charles was shocked. "Last time I saw her they were carting her off into an ambulance and she was dying. I can't believe this. You think Tom messed up?"

"I can only assume Tom did mess up," complained Judy.

"Did you pay him, like we promised?"

"Well, I did skip once, and one time cut him a little short."

"Why?" asked Charles.

"Well, I wanted to make sure, we had enough money for us," said Judy sounding a little worried now, "I thought the special dinner besides all the medicines we were giving Marie, should have done the trick."

"Well, obviously, it didn't," pointed out Charles.

"She's one tough old bird," Judy sounded mad, and tried to think of a solution.

"Even with all the drugs, she's still ticking," said Charles, "I can't believe it. Are you sure it was Marie?"

"Yes, unfortunately," said Judy, "I'm sure. She was with her friend, Ann. That woman who lives in Sedona who came with Marie to Robert's and my wedding. Ann's a retired FBI agent."

"Damn. FBI?" Charles sounded worried.

"And that's not all," said Judy, "they are staying just down the street at the Hilton Hotel, room 306."

"What?"

"I followed them there," Judy reported.

"Well, so what?" said Charles. "We're in Paris, and they can't do anything to us. We didn't do anything that can be proven."

"Well, at least we put all the papers and everything in Roberts' name," Judy confirmed, "and he's gone, out of the way. But I wonder if I left something undone, that I should have done?"

"Well, guess we should have made sure that Marie was out of the way before we took off. Well, we're here in lovely Paris, so let's try to relax," encouraged Charles, "We are probably worrying for nothing."

"I don't like loose ends," said Judy. "It's bad enough we left Tom behind to testify against us; but, now we have Marie to contend with, too.

"Well, come on she's an old lady," said Charles, "we can easily do her in."

"How?" asked Judy, "we sure haven't so far. She's like a damn cat with nine lives."

"Leave that up to me. Tell me exactly where are they staying and you said in room 306?" Charles was thinking up a plan. He could easily break into their room and give Marie a shot, make it look like a heart attack.

"Well, whatever you are planning," worried Judy, "do it quickly."

"Okay, but I'm hungry, that was a small croissant, let's go to dinner, and then take the train to London, like we planned. I'll deal with Marie when we get back."

CHAPTER FIFTY-TWO

Tom enjoyed working in Jack's restaurant. He caught on quickly and liked French cooking. He liked hanging around Jack and getting to know him again.

"You catch on fast," said Jack, as he showed Tom how to make various dishes. Parisians love rich food but they eat smaller portions than Americans, so Tom had to get used to using more butter and making smaller portions. The restaurant was open for lunch and dinner, and business was booming. Tom enjoyed getting to know the other cooks, waitresses, and the hostesses. He felt well-hidden and safe in Paris. Tom spent most of his time either in the restaurant or in his apartment above the restaurant. After a while he even forgot about Judy and Charles. That is, until they showed up one evening for dinner. He couldn't believe his eyes when, he happened to look out from the kitchen as the hostess was seating them at table eleven.

"Tom, come on let's go," warned Jack, "orders are stacking up."

"Oh, hey sure, I got it boss," Tom always called Jack boss, and Jack smiled as he too chipped in and hurriedly prepared orders. Jack helped until he got called away by a food supplier and had to go to his office to write the guy a check.

Tom just happened to get the order for table eleven. His brain went into a tizzy. He wanted to make a mad dash up to his apartment and get the vial of poison mushroom powder hidden in his travel bag. He could easily put it in the soup Judy and Charles ordered; but then if he killed them both, he wouldn't get the money they owed him. *Oh the hell with the money, why shouldn't they get some of their own medicine!*

CHAPTER FIFTY-THREE

"Marie, why did we come here?" asked Ann, "I mean the sights are wonderful and I truly love Paris, but why did you want to come at this time?"

"I really don't know," said Marie, "I guess I had some crazy idea I would see Robert. I know that sounds silly. I was grieving for Robert, I guess. And if I were back at Pleasant View saying something like that, they would move me to the mental ward. Oh, I know Robert is dead. I just still connect Robert with Judy, I guess. I am being silly I know, thinking that if I see Judy, that Robert will be with her." Marie was tearing up.

"Oh, I am so sorry," said Ann sympathetically, and put her hand on Marie's shoulder.

" I know Robert's gone," said Marie reaching for a tissue, "I know he's gone."

"Come on let's take a walk and see some sights, maybe that'll help," suggested Ann.

CHAPTER FIFTY-FOUR

Pete had gotten a photo and prison records of Tom Clark, but he was nowhere to be found. It took Pete a while to figure out that Tom Clark had left the country after his escape. Federal, passport, security tapes and records indicated Tom took a plane to Paris. Realizing that Tom was in Paris as was Charles and Judy gave Pete urgency to join them and rein in all three of them and bring them back to be prosecuted.

Pete took the next flight and arrived in Paris and got a room. He had no idea where to begin looking for Charles and Judy so he did the tourist thing hoping to spot them. He went to all the popular tourist attractions and restaurants. He had an advantage, he knew what they looked like but they had no idea what he looked like. He showed the pictures of Charles, Judy and Tom to the hotel manager where he was staying.

"This one looks slightly familiar," the hotel clerk

managed to say in broken English as he pointed to Tom's photo.

"Have you seen him recently?" asked Pete.

"I believe he was here the other day and asked about this man and a woman."

"These two?" asked Pete, and showed him the pictures again of Charles and Judy.

"Yes, Monsieur."

"Well, if you see him again, or this man and woman, will you let me know?" Pete asked the clerk.

"Of course, Monsieur," the hotel clerk was only two eager to please the American who introduced himself as an investigator.

Pete continued to spend his time taking the tourist routes and asking hotel and store clerks if they had seen Tom or Judy and Charles. After three days, his superior was trying to talk him into coming back to the States, but Pete was determined and felt in his gut he was getting close to finding them. He spent his days walking the streets and visiting shops and museums, the Louvre, the Eiffel Tower. He took bus tours to see the surrounding countryside. He learned a lot about the beautiful city but with no signs of Tom, Charles or Judy. He was going to have to leave soon and head back home there were too many cases waiting for him to work on and his boss was getting impatient.

That evening, close to dinnertime, he came upon an interesting looking restaurant and decided to get something to eat. The hostess sat him near the back, in a rather secluded corner at a window table near the street. He was busy looking at the menu and listening to the waitress list the specials, when he happened to notice a rather interesting couple come in the door and stand near the hostess station.

The woman had lovely red hair, was rather small, and wore lots of bangles and bracelets on both arms. The man she was with was tall and good-looking. They looked familiar. Pete knew it was Judy and Charles without even double-checking the photos he kept in his sport jacket vest pocket. He subconsciously sat back in his chair moving a little closer behind a plant before he reminded himself that Charles and Judy did not know what he looked like.

"I'll have this," said Pete, pointing to an item on the menu he was not quite sure of, certainly did not know how to pronounce the name of the dish, he just pointed to an item with a picture that looked appealing.

"Good choice, Monsieur," the pretty young waitress said with broken English and a lovely French accent. "It's a most popular escargot dish."

"Escargot?" asked Pete. He never ate snails before.

The waitress smiled when she saw his expression, and added, "The dish also comes with broiled chicken with a creamy buttery lemon sauce, with garden potatoes and asparagus." She assured Pete it was most popular.

"That'll be fine, thank you," Pete smiled, he didn't really care, and his thoughts were on watching the red head with the tall guy who was seated across the dining room, practically out of sight. Pete had to rise slightly forward to see around a plant in order to watch them.

It was then when he was stretching his neck and trying to do it discreetly that he noticed a familiar looking face through the open window in the wall to the kitchen. Of course, the cook had on a chef's tall white hat and white chef's coat. This time he pulled the pictures out and sure enough, the chef looked like Tom Clark.

"Holy shit, the whole gangs here," Pete said aloud to himself. His dinner was brought to him about the same time he noticed that Judy and Charles got their dinner. His dinner looked delicious and he was hungry. As he took his first bite a thought suddenly struck him.

If the cook was indeed Tom Clark, and the couple Pete was watching was Judy and Charles—just what was the possibility that Tom cooked Judy and Charles' dinner? He had no proof of anything. Ann had told Pete about Tom cooking something called a blue plate special for Marie, that made her very ill and traces of poison mushrooms were found in her stomach. There was nothing he could do but wait and maybe follow them when they left the restaurant.

CHAPTER FIFTY-FIVE

Tom began to sweat, and not from the heat from the stoves in the kitchen, but from the butterflies he was feeling in the pit of his stomach. He was getting nervous. Jack had left the kitchen to deal with the delivery guy. This was Tom's only chance to get the mushroom powder from his bag in his apartment. Without saying a word, he slipped out and ran up the back steps to his apartment. He knew exactly where his little container with the secret ingredient was hidden. Hurriedly he ran to the closet and reached in his travel bag and grabbed it. With the speed of lightning, he ran back down to the kitchen and continued with table eleven's order.

To be sure it was them, he quickly peered through the opening between the kitchen and the dining once again. Yes, both Judy and Charles were still seated at table eleven. He was nervous to get the dosage just right. He was going to have to use extra strength for the special powder to work fast, but not too fast where Judy and

Charles would pass out right there in the restaurant. He had to use good judgment so they would collapse in their room back at their hotel. What if they didn't go to the hotel? It didn't matter.

He had already added the special toxic ingredients to their soup and sprinkled some in the buttery lemon sauce that topped their lobster bisque. Finished, he rang the bell for the waitress to deliver the dinner to table eleven. Tom was nervous but became distracted with so many more dinner orders that had to be filled that were stacked up behind him. Still, he managed to steal some glances at table eleven once in a while and watch Judy and Charles. They appeared to be enjoying their dinners. *Better enjoy it; it will be your last!*

CHAPTER FIFTY-SIX

Oh my, this lobster is delicious," commented Judy, "I love the buttery lemon sauce."

"This is delicious," Charles said raising his glass of Dom Perignon to make a toast. "Here's to us." Charles touched his glass with Judy's, and they kissed before taking a sip.

"Here's to us," Judy said with a smile.

They talked about future plans as they enjoyed their dinner. They watched the time because they had plans to catch a train yet that evening to travel through the tunnel and tour London where they had a room waiting for them at the Marriott.

They both felt happy and a little light-headed as they left the restaurant and laughed and blamed it on the champagne. They walked arm in arm the short way to the train station. It was a lovely evening in Paris. The lights were stunning, and they felt high.

CHAPTER FIFTY-SEVEN

Pete watched as Charles paid for dinner, and helped Judy with her jacket. He watched them walk out. Pete quickly put his money down on the table got up and headed out the door. But the waitress stopped him to chat and ask about the food. He hurried to answer her questions, made sure he paid enough money not being used to using Francs. The bill paid, he hurried out the door.

Judy and Charles were nowhere to be seen. He had lost them. He had no idea which direction Judy and Charles were headed. He thought they went in the direction to the train station but he wasn't sure. Looking both ways as he stood on the street outside the restaurant he noticed two women walking his way.

"Oh my god, the whole gang sure is here!" Pete said to himself. Then to the ladies approaching him, "Well, hello ladies. Just what are you two doing here?" Pete couldn't believe his eyes "Ann, you didn't tell me, you were coming to Paris."

"It was a last-minute thing," smiled Ann, "a brain storm, I guess you could say," She saw Pete look at Marie.

"Hi," Marie smiled.

"Pete, this is Marie."

"Well, let me give you a hug. I feel I know you already," Marie said.

"My, I figured you were Marie," said Pete, "you look well after all you have been through."

"Yes, I'm pretty tough."

"So, really, what are you ladies up to?" asked Pete.

"We are looking to get something to eat," shared Ann, "is this a good place?"

"Well, I just ate here, and the food was delicious."

"Oh, you don't say," said Marie, "sure smells good here."

"This was delicious, but I think you should try the restaurant I went to last evening," suggested Pete., "It's just right around the corner near the train station. Come, I'll show you."

Ann and Marie looked at each other and nodded in agreement. They began to walk with Pete toward the train station.

"Where are you ladies staying?" asked Pete.

"Oh, we are right around the corner and down the street, at the Hilton," Marie replied.

"It's a wonder we haven't run into each other before now," smiled Pete, "that is exactly where I am staying." Pete did not tell the ladies that he saw Judy and Charles and was about to follow them. They were long gone. He would have to start all over again trying to find them.

Pete also forgot the idea that Tom the chef might have tried to poison Judy and Charles. He just forgot the whole incident as Marie, Ann and he began chit chatting about the sights they had visited in Paris. They ended up having a lovely evening at the restaurant Pete suggested. Having already had dinner, Pete enjoyed wine and conversation with them as they enjoyed their meal and then had dessert with them. Charles and Judy were forgotten for the evening.

CHAPTER FIFTY-EIGHT

Tom wondered what ever happened to Judy and Charles. They certainly left the restaurant looking okay. He wondered how far they got before they collapsed into a sickening stupor as all body systems began to shut down. Tom went about working in the kitchen. The place was popular and kept him very busy.

In his own sick mind, he hoped that Judy and Charles enjoyed his cooking while they visited his restaurant. As the chef he was, he was curious, and wondered if Judy and Charles had approved of his lobster dish that he had perfected with creamy buttery lemon sauce. He had peeped through the opening from the kitchen as he worked and seen that they had ate everything on their plates. The restaurant got so busy then that he didn't have time to think about it anymore.

CHAPTER FIFTY-NINE

"My, that train ride," said Judy, "made me kind of sick, and I don't usually get motion sickness."

"Well, it was a fast train, and those flashing lights in the tunnel kind of made me queasy, too," Charles said holding his churning stomach.

Come on, let's check in and get to our room," said Judy, as they were in front of the Marriott in beautiful London. "We'll see the sights tomorrow."

The check in was quick and smooth, as the clerk was expecting Mr. and Mrs. Smith. Charles had decided to use another alias as they were paying with cash.

They were glad to get their room keys and get in to lie down on the bed. They were so tired and sick to their stomachs that they put the "do not disturb" on the door. Too sick and too tired to undress, they laid on the bed with their clothes on. They laid down holding hands neither realizing that they were dying.

"Maybe we drank too much champagne," whispered Charles.

"Well, you know I always get what I want," smiled Judy, "and I wanted a lot of champagne, didn't I?"

"Love you," smiled Charles feeling oozing and sleepy at the same time.

"Love you, too," Judy said and closed her eyes.

It was the last thing that both of them said before they lost consciousness and died a few minutes later.

Two days passed; the "do not disturb" sign remained on the hotel door. Finally, it was the end of Judy and Charles' scheduled stay and past the late checkout time. The maid noticed the "do not disturb sign" still on the door and updated the assistant manager who went to knock on the door.

When there was no answer he used the hotel master key and went into the hotel suite. There in the bedroom he found the two bodies of Mr. And Mrs. Smith lying on the bed holding hands. The police were called. The deaths appeared to them as perhaps a double suicide. The bodies were taken to the morgue as their belongings were searched to see if there were clues for notification of next of kin. All they found was an empty vial in Charles' sport coat pocket.

Judy and Charles met their demise, just as Robert had. Was it karma or just plain greed that did them in? Their evil doings of poisoning people, over-dosing them with strong medicines, and stealing their life savings caught up with them. To do wrong to others was in the end, to do harm to you.

Just as in Robert's sudden death in a fiery car crash, Charles and Judy had no time to repent or to reverse their wrong-doings to all those senior citizens who lived at Pleasant View. Forgiveness, if it was to be considered had to be done on the other side now.

Judy and Charles true identification was never found by the Paris police so they were kept in the morgue for a certain period of time determined by the court of law to see if anyone would come to claim the bodies. The London and Paris newspapers had the story. The article headline read: Charles and Judy Smith apparent murder suicide bodies found in hotel.

Tom learned of his successful murder of Judy and Charles when he picked up the newspaper from the corner stand. The last name wasn't correct; but in his mind he knew the deaths were of Judy and Charles who ran Pleasant View.

The article indicated it appeared to be a double-suicide. Tom figured either the London police did not want to put much into this since the death was of two Americans. Tom knew that the London Police would notify the American Embassy that would notify the FBI. Tom knew that the FBI would eventually investigate further. He smiled to himself as he put the newspaper in the trash and went to work in the kitchen.

CHAPTER SIXTY

"Do you think this couple that committed a double suicide is Judy and Charles?" asked Marie.

"What would be the odds of that?" asked Ann.

"Well, it reads here that their names were Judy and Charles," said Marie adding, "what are the odds of that?"

"It sure is a coincidence," said Ann not totally convinced, but had to admit that the more she thought about it the more it made sense. It was the fact that they were poisoned that caught her attention.

"Yes, what a coincidence!" echoed Marie. Thinking how people at Pleasant View had been deliberately poisoned. She looked at Ann who happened to have been thinking the exact same thing.

"I know what you are thinking, it's the fact that they were poisoned."

"I don't know about Charles, but I can't believe greedy Judy would steal all of that money and not want to live to spend it," shared Marie looking at Ann knowing she had to think the same thing.

"I guess we'll never know what really happened," admitted Ann.

"Well there is nothing we can do here," said Ann, "so are you ready to go back home?"

"Yes, I believe that I am. I like the sound of that, you and I saying home and meaning the same home."

"Me too," smiled Ann.

"Well, we have a flight to New York in the morning," said Marie "how about one last dinner out in a nice restaurant this evening?"

"Sounds good to me," said Ann.

"How about that restaurant where we met Pete?" said Marie. "We haven't had a chance to try that one."

"I wonder if Pete is still here in Paris?" said Ann. She called down at the desk and asked the clerk if Pete Sanders was still at the hotel. The clerk said he was and rang his room. Pete was in and agreed to meet them in the lobby at five.

***

"There you ladies are," said Pete, as he walked up and hugged Ann, then Marie.

"We weren't sure if you were still in Paris," said Marie.

"I may stay a couple more days," shared Pete, "especially since I read the article in this morning's paper about the double-suicide." Pete didn't know if he should express his sympathy to Marie about it possibly being her daughter-in-law that was dead. Marie and Ann acknowledged that they saw the article too, and Marie seemed to be doing okay. So, Pete quickly forgot about saying anything to Marie about her daughter-in-law, especially since Judy was behind the entire goings on that put Marie's life in jeopardy.

"Oh, I see," said Ann "have you learned anything more about a possible identification."

"No, I can't say that I have," said Pete.

"Yes, it's the poisoning angle that made me think of the possibility of the deceased couple being Judy and Charles."

"Yes, me too," said Ann.

"Where do you ladies want to eat?" asked Pete.

"We want to go to the restaurant we saw you coming out of the other night."

"Oh, good choice," said Pete, "sounds good to me." Pete tapped his inside vest pocket of his jacket. Yeah the picture of Tom Clark was still in his pocket. He wanted to make sure that if the same cook was there that it was Tom.

They walked a few blocks to the restaurant. The hostess seated them at a nice table. Pete noticed, but said nothing, that it was the same table that he had seen Judy and Charles sitting at a few days before on the evening that they died lying on the bed in their hotel room.

Could Tom had recognized them and poisoned their dinner? He thought of Tom possibly cooking Judy and Charles dinner that night and adding his special ingredients like he did when he cooked meals at Pleasant View. Pete was actually sort of amazed and wondered how Tom knew the correct dosage that would cause a delay and work slowly and not cause Judy and Charles to collapse in the restaurant. Pete thought it was pretty genius of Tom if it was indeed a timed poisoning.

Pete, Marie and Ann had looked over the menu and were ready to order when the waitress came to their table. Pete had a direct view into the kitchen window from where he was sitting; Ann was across from him and had to turn a slight left to see in the window. Pete spotted Tom working in the kitchen. Even with his chef hat on he knew the guy in the kitchen matched the guy in the photo he had in the pocket of his sport jacket.

Pete could not help but wonder what would happen next. He certainly was not going to eat anything that was brought to their table and he would stop Ann and Marie from eating the food as well. Instead, he would find a way to get them to take the food with them and he could take samples to the lab.

While they were waiting for their food orders to arrive Pete, received an urgent call on his official cellular phone, telling him that the London morgue did perform an autopsy, and found traces of a type of toxic mushroom called Amanita Phalloides in Judy and Charles alias Albright, alias Smith's organs and tissue.

"Sorry about that, ladies," said Pete when he returned from taking his call outside on the street. He was only going to tell the ladies part of what was said in the phone call; not the part about the autopsy or the fact that he saw Judy and Charles ate their last meal and the very same restaurant and table, they were sitting at right now. He didn't want them looking around or becoming alarmed, so did not tell them that Tom would probably be cooking their dinner.

Without saying anything, Ann looked at Pete rather curiously, the result of having been an FBI partner with Ann for years. Pete knew that familiar look and answered her unspoken question.

"It was the Bureau, seems the FBI got a trace on Judy and Charles' money link to Sweden. They are checking files and records and photos, and yes the couple found dead from poisoning was Judy and Charles, apparently."

"Well, I wondered," confessed Ann.

Marie just nodded and looked about the crowded dining room. Pete watched her look towards the kitchen and was surprised she did not say anything about the cook with the chef hat looking familiar. Ann had not said anything either. But then of course they were away from Pleasant View and had no idea Tom was in Paris. Tom would have certainly recognized Ann who he trained and who worked with him in the kitchen at Pleasant View.

Funny, how everyone came to Paris and settled in the same small area. Of course, Pete figured Tom followed Judy and Charles to Paris. Perhaps Judy owed Tom money for his food poisoning services.

Waiting for their food to arrive at the table, Pete, Ann

and Marie engaged in casual conversation mostly about the sights of Paris. Pete asked them about their travel plans to return home just as their food was delivered to their table.

Pete had to think very fast because Ann and Marie were both carrying on about the beautiful presentation and delicious smelling aromas rising up from the dinner plates. He wished he would have had the foresight to clue Marie and Ann in his plan about getting the order to go after it was brought to the table because he figured Tom cooked it and probably poisoned it; but, he feared if he brought it up in the restaurant that their surprised expressions as they looked towards the kitchen would have tipped off Tom.

Pete wanted to catch Tom in the act. As it was, Pete had to be careful that the waitress did not take the plates back into the kitchen to put the food into containers. He had to be careful with is words. He stopped the waitress as she walked by their table.

"Oh, miss, would you bring us three containers and the bill, so we can take this with us. I just received an important telephone call and we have to leave," said Pete as he first glanced at the waitress, and saw Marie and Ann look at each other, then at him.

Ann was a retired FBI agent and used to secretly and scheming and so therefore knew enough to keep quiet. Marie, on the other hand, was about to say something as she picked up her fork. Pete noticed Ann must have bumped her knee and Marie quickly put the fork down and did not finish what she was going to say.

Pete drew a sigh of relief when he saw Marie and Ann were cooperating, as was the waitress who said that she would be back shortly with their containers. Pete was glad it went that way with the waitress because he wanted the verbal transaction to go smoothly. He saw Tom watching them from the kitchen opening in the wall.

CHAPTER SIXTY-ONE

Tom didn't know if he should be nervous or not. He was only too glad that he had enough "special ingredient" to sprinkle on the three dinners. *Yeah why not get rid of all of them?* he thought, *that way there would be no witnesses, or anyone to testify against him.* Tom had read the newspaper and he knew his secret ingredient was just toxic enough and took along enough to take effect so Judy and Charles would be far enough away when they collapsed, so as to not implicate the restaurant or him.

He was a genius at this. Something he had come up with himself as a teenager after poisoning his child-abusing sick-in-the-head uncle by doctoring his daily six packs of beer with anti-freeze. Something sinister happened to Tom after he poisoned his uncle. He found that the act had been easy and he had no remorse. Of course, the evil deed got him juvenile court and he had to serve jail time, but it was worth it.

Later, Tom served as a cook in Viet Nam and that was where he learned about slow acting toxic Amanita Phalloides "death cap" mushrooms from a fellow soldier, Bob, who was from northern California and loved to hunt wild mushrooms. Bob had learned the hard way, which ones to take home and eat and which ones, the poison ones, to leave in the forest.

One day while hunting for morels, the good ones, he didn't find enough of them, so thinking that all wild mushrooms were safe to eat, he tried some that looked a little different. He soon found out he was wrong when after a couple of hours he got deathly ill, was rushed to the hospital where he nearly died. Tom had made a mental note of Bob's story, and what the mushrooms were called, what they looked like, and where to find them.

Tom liked living in Paris; he was enjoying himself and his co-workers. He loved joking with the waitresses and he had a crush on his buddy Jack. The way Jack responded to him, he knew that sooner or later he and Jack would be one. They had flirted with each other and had a secret relationship while serving as cooks in Vietnam. The makeshift tent kitchen was hot and steaming as was their late afternoon secret sexual encounters.

Tom did not think about the consequences or how his actions would affect Jack. There could be a disastrous outcome if Tom's toxic habit of poisoning people would come out in the open. Tom knew he had to be extra careful. He knew he got the portions correct because it worked so well with Judy and Charles.

It gave him pleasure to poison her and her high and mighty attitude. Sure, she owed him money but she was also a witness to his wrong doings and so she deserved to be poisoned. All went well with getting rid of Judy and Charles and so he hoped this event would go well too. But, he worried when he saw the waitress deliver carry-out containers to table eleven. Oh well, so what if they decided to eat his delicious cooking somewhere else—like back at their hotel.

My god, who else would walk into the restaurant from Pleasant View? Robert? And then he remembered that Robert died in a fiery car crash. Oh he knew Judy was behind Robert's death. He had heard the rumors and looked up back newspaper articles and learned that Judy's first husband, Roger Blake, also died in a car accident of the same sort—running off a cliff and down an embankment much the same way that Robert's car flew off a mountain side into an Arizona canyon.

CHAPTER SIXTY-TWO

"Well, that was sudden," exclaimed Marie as they used their forks to slide the food from the plates into the to-go containers and hurried out the door. Marie was about to drool, the food smelled so delicious. She wanted to dig into the plate of French delight; but then she realized that perhaps Pete was quickly steering them out of the restaurant for a reason. So, she settled into accepting the fast changes and tactics of these two FBI agents.

She came to realize that she liked the cloak and dagger spy angle of these two comrades in her company. Maybe I would have become an FBI agent too, if I hadn't met Frank and gotten pregnant. She smiled thinking, you can't change the past, but was glad to be able to participate into secrecy and intrigue even if her life had been threatened at Pleasant View. Marie's mind returned to the here and now, as she and Ann got up to follow Pete out the door.

"Come on let's get out of here," said Ann as they left the restaurant had headed down the street. As they walked Pete explained his unusual behavior and why they could not eat their food.

"Where to, next?" asked Marie.

"Let's go back to the hotel," said Pete. I want to get these samples to a safe place and put them in my hotel room refrigerator. They will be safe there until I can contact the bureau's lab in the morning.

They hurried off to Pete's hotel room, put the dinners in the refrigerator, and headed to another nice Parisian restaurant that Pete had gone earlier in the week.

"I love French cuisine," Marie sighed as she was grateful for finally getting to eat.

"Pete, have you looked into the kitchen?" Marie had to ask. "Hopefully Tom doesn't work here, too," Marie joked in between bites. Her attempt at joking did not get past Ann and Pete. They had to chuckle because what were the chances of being possible victims of attempted poisoning twice in one evening?

"Yes, we can't lose our sense of humor," said Ann "besides soon all this well be behind us." She looked at Marie and Pete now and wondered what they were thinking.

"So, what is your next step, Pete?" asked Ann.

"Well, I'll keep a tab on Tom while I wait for the lab test results to come back." He replied, and took another bite of his dinner of fish with a simple butter base Beurre Blanc sauce.

"So glad you spotted Tom at the restaurant," said Marie.

"I suspect the test results will be positive," said Ann.

"But don't you need a sample of the poison to come from his possession?" asked Marie beginning to sound like an FBI agent herself. "I mean don't you need to find it in his possession, otherwise he could say it was someone else who poisoned those people?"

"Well, we'll see," said Pete, in the meantime he was wondering how he could search through Tom's things and wondered, too, what if he had no more of the toxic substance left in his procession? All he needed was a small amount to nail Tom. Even just a bit of toxic dust from a container in his possession would be enough for the authorities to nab him.

So Pete set out to plan his next scheme. Another agent was watching Tom's whereabouts for Pete and reported that Tom stayed in a small apartment above the kitchen of the Jack's restaurant where he worked. Pete would have his associate keep an eye on Tom as he worked in the kitchen and he would sneak up to search his apartment. Pete got the call from the lab with the results right after he saw Ann and Marie off to the airport.

They were flying into New York then on to Phoenix, on their way home to Sedona. It was time for Marie to settle down and enjoy peaceful surroundings with Ann and try to put all of the turmoil of Pleasant View behind them. Marie was doing better and accepting the fact that Robert was gone. It wasn't easy for her to realize how Robert got mixed up with Judy. They were both gone now.

It would be a long time before Marie would get over her traumatic stay at Pleasant View. The senior living center's new operators were being closely monitored by the state to make sure the new proprietors were proportioning medicines correctly, and not over prescribing them. Workers and cooks were vetted closely and monitored to make sure no wrongdoing was going on as before. And residents' money was watched more closely as well. Residents were paying monthly and no longer offered and talked into portfolio investment by Pleasant View.

CHAPTER SIXTY-THREE

Pete got the lab results back and yes, the food that they were served in the restaurant where Tom cooked had been tampered with and tainted with traces of toxic Amanita Phalloides mushrooms. So, Pete made arrangements with another agent to visit the restaurant when Tom was cooking. The plan was for Pete to sneak into Tom's apartment and search it while Jim, his associate, kept an eye on Tom while eating at the restaurant.

Jim was not afraid to eat there, because he was excited to use a new FBI toxic meter device that the bureau recently acquired. It was state of the art technology that tested foods for toxins and gave instant results. It was a pocket-sized syringe device with a small analog meter. It the meter went into the red zone, it meant there were traces of a toxic material. While Pete searched Tom's apartment, it was Jim's job was to keep an eye on Tom.

Jim sat at table eleven in hopes that Tom would be

cooking his food. But first Pete was going to have to make Jim seem like a suspicious character that Tom might want to dispose of. So, Pete sent Jim to the restaurant a day or two earlier to question Tom.

CHAPTER SIXTY-FOUR

Jim entered the restaurant and asked the hostess if he could speak with the manager. He waited only a minute before the hostess returned with Jack following close behind her. Jim introduced himself.

"Hello," smiled Jack, "how can I help you?"

Jack confirmed that he was the manager then asked to speak with Tom Clark, the cook. Jack seemed curious but was happy to oblige and went to get Tom. Of course, Jack wondered and was eager to ask Tom why the FBI had to come and question him. Tom was busy, but it was after lunchtime and orders were slowing down.

"There's an FBI guy, here to talk to you," Jack said with a worried look on his face.

"Me?" asked Tom trying to act innocent and not nervous, but his stomach was beginning to tighten up in nervous knots.

"So, what's you been up to," asked Jack "are you in some kind of trouble? Is that why you came back to me, so you could hide out?" Jack was getting suspicious and worried that he was only being used.

"No, no such thing!" Tom tried to sound innocent and sincere. "I have no idea why he is here." Tom lied, of course. He knew why an FBI agent would want to question him. His first impulse was to bolt out the kitchen door and get as far away from there as possible. But, he knew he had to talk to the guy, hopefully it was all a mistake, but he doubted it. Still, he could not run, for some reason he could not explain, he feet were planted right there next to Jack. This was where he wanted to stay, and work right alongside Jack. Tom tried to avoid Jack's worried eyes as he walked pass him to go meet with the FBI agent.

"Are you Tom Clark?" asked Jim showing Tom his FBI identification badge.

"Yes, I am," said Tom. "What's going on?"

"Did you work at Pleasant View Senior Living Center?" asked Jim. Talking slow trying to stall as long as he could. He was trying to give Pete as much time as he could in order to get in and search Tom's apartment for toxicity evidence.

"I just wanted to ask you a few questions regarding Judy Dems and Dr. Charles Allen and Pleasant View Senior Living Center," said Jim looking Tom up and down as if he expected him of wrongdoing. Jim watched Tom appear relaxed as he ran his fingers to his thick curly hair. Tom held his thin long body tall and proud. He had nothing to hide.

"Well, I was a cook at Pleasant View," offered Tom.

He was surprised that he wasn't a bit nervous but confidant. He figured he did not do anything wrong because Judy and Charles were bad people—just like his sexual abusive uncle was a bad person and needed to be dealt with.

"Did you notice any suspicious goings on while you worked there?" asked Jim. The whole point of Jim's inquiry was to keep Tom busy while Pete was snooping around, so Jim did not question him too intently. He did not want to accuse him of anything to scare him off, so he just questioned him regarding Judy and Charles.

"No, I can't say that I did," smiled Tom, feeling pretty confident, "of course I spent most of my time in the kitchen. I only knew Judy Dems on a business level and only knew Dr. Charles Allen by seeing him there at Pleasant View."

"Well, okay then," said Pete "and you never overheard any rumors about families feeling they were getting their inheritance ripped off?" Jim was careful and kept the questioning only to monetary matters. And when he felt that Pete probably had enough time to snoop around in Tom's apartment, he ended the visit with Tom and let him get back to work. The idea was not to spook him only to keep him occupied for a few minutes.

"Anything else?" asked Tom.

"No that's it, thank you for your time," said Jim "sure smells good in here and I haven't had lunch. What do you recommend?"

"Oh, my grilled salmon is to die for," Tom also

chuckled out loud realizing what he just said. He caught himself then went on, "the buttery sauce is made with an au sec Chablis for a deliciously luxurious Beurre blend." Tom smiled and pointed to the dining area.

"Why not have a seat at the table over there and I'll cook you up something really special?" Tom pointed to table eleven and Jim's stomach took a nervous flip.

"Great, sure will," smiled Jim as he turned to head to the table Tom had pointed out.

"Won't be long; you are going to love my salmon," smiled Tom reaching into his pocket to pull out a small container.

"Sounds delicious, can't wait," smiled Jim. Jim was feeling a little nervous. His hand moved in his jacket pocket to make sure the syringe toxic meter was still there—it was. Jim sat quietly and looked around the restaurant wondering how Pete's search was going.

He only had to wait a few more minutes, till she saw Pete standing outside looking in the window at him. Jim raised his finger in acknowledgement. Shortly after, the waitress brought his salmon dinner to his table. It looked delicious and smelled wonderful. Jim was so hungry that he had to use all of his will power not to pick up the fork and dig in.

Instead, he looked towards the kitchen and spotted Tom who was busy doing something and talking to another cook. So, Jim quickly pulled out his syringe and poked the needle in several places to draw up samples. It was a good thing that the meter did not have bells and whistles, because the meter's needle quickly shot over to the red zone indicating full toxicity. Jim was astonished that the meter was going practically off the screen — reaching way over to the highly toxic range.

Jim looked up and signaled to Pete to let him know he found toxicity. He saw Pete nod as if he had found evidence too. Jim put his meter syringe away and signaled to the waitress to bring him a carry out box. He quickly slid the food from the plate to the container, covered it up and held on to it tight. There was enough evidence here to put Tom away for a very long time.

Pete came in and Jim joined him and they went to the kitchen to arrest Tom. Tom had a sinking feeling right away when he added the poison to the dinner that he was doomed. But he just couldn't resist poisoning the FBI agent's food.

Pete ordered Tom to turn around and put his arms behind his back then he snapped cuffs on him. Tom went peacefully, walking right past Jack, who stood in the doorway looking wide eyed, with mixed emotions of anger and grief. His mouth gaped open, not knowing what to say as Tom walked away with the two FBI agents. Tom kept his head down leaving Jack without explanation, as he felt no remorse.

A short time passed, Tom had a speedy trial. He was found guilty and was sentenced to life in prison. There his talents did not go without reward. Of all places, they put him to work in the kitchen where he became the head chef, and the prison gang assassin-by-toxicity expert. That worked out well for about two years until he met his own demise, when an opposing gang leader stabbed him in the neck with a makeshift knife and he bled to death.

***

Pleasant View was released by the state and bought by another senior living center firm. The money Judy and Charles had sent to a Swiss Bank was retrieved and families who had lost loved ones got their share of the money they were supposed to get.

In the end, Marie lost her son and daughter-in-law but gained millions in life insurance money that Judy had on Robert and that Robert had on Judy. Marie had to come to terms with the tragedy in her life of losing her son. But moving in with Ann and living among the red rocks with its many spiritual vortexes connecting souls with the universe, helped immensely.

"Come on, you can do it," joked Marie as she staggered up the mountainside ahead of Ann.

"Slow up, will you," complained Ann with a grin. She was only happy to see Marie back to her old self and having much more energy than Ann thought she ever had.

"I'll sit over here and wait for you," laughed Marie, spotting a nice flat rock where they could sit and eat the lunch they brought with them.

"I'll be there in a minute, don't eat mine," said Ann trying to laugh while breathing hard and wishing Marie wouldn't always pick the toughest climbs when it was her turn to choose. Still, she loved the challenge and she loved giving Marie the opportunity to feel so much stronger than herself. Giving Marie bragging rights was well worth the struggle to keep up with her.

Ann had seen Marie at her lowest point when Robert, Judy, Charles and Tom had her doped up with lots of medicines and bad food. Back then, she never would have imagined that she would see her friend so revitalized and rejuvenated after all that she had been through. Ann felt very fortunate and smiled as Marie bent over and stretched out her hand to help her best friend climb over that last big stone to reach the top rock at Boynton Canyon. There, physically fit and ultra-efficient, Marie had already spread a small blanket with lunch all set up.

"Love you," was all Marie said after she pulled Ann near and gave her a big hug.

"Love you too, speedy," laughed Ann.

"Come on let's eat," suggested Marie, "I got another hike planned for around Bell Rock when we are finished with lunch."

"What?" Ann sighed as Marie laughed and handed her a sandwich.

"Just kidding," said Marie and they both laughed appreciating life, their friendship and their beautiful surroundings.

"Now that's a pleasant view," sighed Marie as they sat and ate lunch and looked out among the Red Rocks.

"Yes, it is," smiled Ann, "certainly is a pleasant view."

About the Author

This is Dianne Zimmermann's fourth novel. Her other books are *Emma's Run, Jane's Aliens, Hooch Runners*, published by BookCrafters. Dianne lives in St. Louis and enjoys writing, drawing, photography, running, hiking and road trips.